A Valentine for a Vet

Carolyn Miller

ONE

The rustic charm and grace of Three Creek Ranch had never felt so far away. Dr. Jessica James, veterinarian, pulled up outside the swanky mansion, all modern architectural lines and landscaping that screamed money, style and pretension, a thousand times removed from the humble wooden farmhouse she called home. She braced, knowing she had to exude professionalism, seeing as she'd been sent here by her boss, Dr. Theodore Ramesky, for the first time.

"The Mellencamps are important clients, Jessie, and we need to do all we can to help them."

In other words, *keep these guys happy if you want to keep your job.*

She pressed her lips together. Exactly why she'd signed up for veterinary school. To cater to the rich, at the expense of the poorer clients who had booked to see her, and now would be waiting hours longer, unless they were seen by one of her equally long-suffering colleagues.

Oh well. As the youngest veterinarian on the Ramesky Veterinary Clinic books she had to do what Theo said, even if a lot of his reckonings seemed more about keeping up appearances rather than doing the actual work of the veterinary practice she'd studied so long and hard for.

She retrieved her bag then closed the door of her humble Nissan, then moved to press the buzzer on the gate. Giselle Mellencamp was expecting her, or so Theo had said.

"Hello, it's Dr. James, here to see about a Pekinese." Her nose wrinkled. Her favorite type of dog.

There was no response, but the gates slowly opened, which was reply enough. As she walked up the stenciled concrete driveway, she noted the silver Porsche sitting in front of the garage, its sleek lines making her own boxy car look like someone's maiden aunt dressed in eighties clothes. Still, her car worked and got her from A to B, so a girl couldn't be too fussy. Especially a girl who had spent so much on her studies and could only afford the most basic type of vehicle.

She lifted a hand to knock on the huge glass-paned entrance, but before she could knock a yapping was accompanied by the arrival of a pink fluffball. Yes, pink. Her heart fell. Didn't people know that dogs were living, sentient creatures? Dyeing them for entertainment sent the message that dogs were objects or toys, which went against everything she believed in.

But, judging from the woman who sashayed into view, whose appearance held every bit of sleek Instagram-worthiness as the car outside, it felt like those objections would fall on deaf ears. Pink highlights, the exact color of the dog's coat, filled the woman's tresses in what Jess's sister Poppy would probably call a balayage.

Lord, help me not judge. She found a smile. "Hi. I'm Dr. James."

The blonde trailed a hot pink fake nail through her curls, her heavily mascaraed lashes widening as she lifted her eyebrows. "*You're* Dr. James?"

Hadn't she just said that? "Yes. I'm here to see—"

"I was expecting someone male... and older."

Ah, another one of those clients, then. The type who thought because Jess was young that she was dumb. She'd battled that since taking on her role as a new graduate in the practice last year. The best way to deal with that was to prove herself a professional.

She dropped her smile. "I'm here to see Henrietta."

The woman bent low, flashing cleavage, and scooped up the yappy pink puppy. "This is Henrietta. Isn't she the sweetest?"

"She's certainly got a good set of lungs on her."

The caterpillar lashes squeezed together in a narrowed gaze that might make a lesser mortal squirm. But not for nothing had Jess dealt with two sisters and a brother, and fought the stereotypes that had seen her graduate as one of only two females in her class. She braced within. She'd always hated when people didn't introduce themselves. And she'd learned the hard way that not everyone who answered the door had the responsibility of the animal in question. "I'm assuming you are Giselle Mellencamp?"

"Yes." More eyelash fluttering. "Don't you recognize me?"

"No." Should she? Was she an influencer or something?

"Oh. I thought everyone in town knew me." She shrugged. "Everyone who knows anyone knows, I suppose."

Now probably wasn't the time to tell this woman that her brother played for Calgary's NHL team and her sister-in-law just so happened to be one of the leading sports reporters on ESPN. "What is it you do?" she asked, as sweetly as she could, as Giselle invited her inside.

"I'm an influencer."

Bingo.

"I dabble in makeup and fashion."

She sure did. Although 'dabbling' might be an understatement. "Okay, well, what seems to be the problem with Henrietta?" Apart from the pinkness. She was sorely tempted to ask if she was dyed with non-toxic dye, but kept her lips closed as Theo's implied words sang in her mind: *Keep the clients happy.*

"Well, as you can see, Henrietta was at the groomers recently —just yesterday, in fact. But since she's come home she's acting a little agitated."

"May I?" She reached for the dog.

Henrietta growled, so Jess reached for a treat from the ever-present plastic pouch stashed in her pocket. Henrietta sniffed it, then decided Jess could be friend, not foe, and ate it. She trotted over as Jess knelt and held out another one.

As Henrietta chewed, Jess ran expert hands over the small dog's body. "I can't feel anything out of the ordinary." She glanced up. "How is she acting agitated?"

Giselle shrugged. "She's just a little snippy with me. She vomited too." She shuddered. "It was so gross."

Her heart tensed. "Vomiting can be a sign that they are reacting to something they've ingested."

"But she hasn't eaten anything different," Giselle whined.

"Ingested, not digested." Jess peered more closely at the dog's coat. Oh no. She glanced up sharply. "What kind of dye was used by the groomer?"

Giselle waved a hand. "It can't be the dye. Everything is natural. Besides, you just said it was something she ate."

"No. I said it might be something she ingested. Something that her skin has come into contact with. The chemicals used in many human products, especially hair dye, are extremely toxic to dogs and can cause serious illness, as well as cause severe skin and coat issues."

"But it's *natural*."

"Was the dye designed for dogs? Dogs have a very different pH level of their skin to humans which is why products that come into contact need to be toxin free. What was used?"

"I can't remember the specific ingredients, but they *are* all natural," Giselle insisted.

Jess stood, holding the dog. Poor pooch. "Well, if you don't remember, your dog may become very ill very quickly. You need to find out from the groomer what was used in the dye. Now."

Giselle swore. "Fine. I'll go get the packet."

Henrietta whined after her, which caused Giselle to pause. "Mommy will be right back. Love you, Honeybun."

Mommy didn't love Henrietta if she'd done what Jess thought

she had. *Lord, please give me grace and wisdom.* It wasn't the dog's fault she had an owner who was either clueless or didn't care.

Giselle soon stalked back, and sullenly handed Jess a dye box that had Giselle's own face plastered on the front.

Yep, just as she'd suspected. "This is human dye."

"It's safe. It's all natural."

"Since when is pink a natural color on dogs?"

Giselle swore again. "Wow. So harsh. You don't have to be so blunt."

Unfortunately, blunt seemed to be as much a part of her DNA as loving animals was. All her life she had dealt with those who delighted in calling her Jessie James, after the famous western gun-slinger and sharp-shooter. Direct was what she did. "I'm not here to waste time on telling you lies. Your dog is sick, and may possibly die, all because you wanted to make a beauty statement."

"Don't you dare judge me!"

Heat roared within. "I'm a vet. I have a degree that says I'm entitled to make a judgement based on the treatment of the animals within my care."

"Well, Henrietta is not in your care." Giselle snatched the dog away. "Not anymore."

"Dr. Theodore—"

"Will be hearing about your inexpert care. I can't believe you think you know better than I do about what's best for Henrietta."

"And yet you were the one calling for advice from a vet."

"I'm going to report you."

"For what? For caring about whether your dog lives?" Jess took a deep breath. That's right. Right now wasn't about who was right or wrong. This dog might well not make it unless Giselle saw sense. "Henrietta needs to be treated. Already her skin is blistering. You can see that on her front right leg."

"Where?"

"See?" Jess pointed to the section of skin near the right knee. "And I suspect she will vomit again. Dogs lick their coats, so she's probably got some of that poison in her system. She may even have internal burns."

"What?" Giselle's shriek bounced off the white tiles. "So what do I do?"

"I have some charcoal tablets which will help absorb any poison inside. And she'll need to have her hair shaved off so we can treat any burns."

"But she'll look so ugly."

"Do you want her to live?"

"You really need to work on your people skills," Giselle muttered.

Not the only one. But there was a reason she'd chosen veterinary medicine instead of human medicine. And her lack of patience with people might have come into it. "I need to take her with me so I can get her started on pain meds and get her cleaned up."

"But my groomer—"

"Yes, give me their number. Because your groomer should be banned from ever treating dogs again if they don't know the difference between using human and dog friendly products. And if they do, and they were coerced to ignore the difference, then perhaps you should be prohibited from ever owning another dog again."

Giselle gasped, but Jess didn't have time for her theatrics. "Come on, Henrietta. Let's get you somewhere safe."

"Somewhere safe?" Another shriek bounced off the walls. "I'm her *mother*."

"No. You're her human owner. You're supposed to be an adult, but you've made your dog your toy. I'll be having words with Dr. Theodore about whether you should be holding a registration for a dog license."

"You can't do that!"

"Watch me."

.   .   .

By the time she returned to the clinic, handed poor Henrietta over to the vet clinic's head nurse who winced then crooned over the dog as if she was her own, Jess was exhausted. Yet she still had to clean up the vomit in the car—sure enough, the crate hadn't contained it all—and complain to Dr. Theodore, who would *not* be pleased with how things had progressed. Then do her catch up with her other patients, before her dog obedience class tonight.

It might seem a little strange that a qualified vet was running these classes, but Dr. Theodore insisted it gave their practice greater credibility, that those who came appreciated the qualified nature of the instructor. And seeing this was something Jess had done to supplement her income during her studies, she was prepared to prove herself a team player and do the classes still. Especially as it brought in more dollars. And, she suspected, after today's debacle, she would likely have to prove herself team player-like all the more.

She just hoped that the owners tonight would have the right attitude towards their pets, and not treat them as accessories or toys. And that maybe she could find her footing again, after the unpleasantness of before.

Her head thumped with another of the headaches that had started two months after her accepting the role at Ramesky Veterinary Clinic. She loved animals, loved to see them thrive, and had been thrilled to get this position upon graduating two years ago, and she hoped she'd done enough to save Henrietta from her owner's cluelessness. But sometimes the stress this job involved meant this job didn't love Jess at all.

"Come on, Benji. Down." Tom Chavez pointed and his Labrador instantly obeyed. "Good boy." He rubbed his head, fed him a treat. "Okay, are you ready to surprise her?"

Benji woofed, which he took as a yes.

He sure hoped Jessica James would take it as a nice surprise.

Ever since the season had ended in round one of the playoffs, he'd been wracking his brain trying to think of how to finally stay in her circle of acquaintances. The hockey season was usually pretty good at seeing her attend the occasional game to watch her brother, Franklin. Each time she did Tom would be sure to play just a bit better, a bit harder, in the hopes that she'd notice him. And while they'd talked and even danced at Franklin's wedding last year—the highlight of Tom's year—he wanted more.

She might be his teammate's sister, but she was funny, spunky, smart as heck, and pretty to boot. The fact she was a Christian put the puck in the back of the net. She was his ideal woman, even if Franklin had looked askance at him a time or two when he'd caught them talking.

So when he'd overheard Jess say that she was running dog training classes at her veterinary clinic, it was an easy yes. Hence he was here. And so was his already trained Benji, his wingman, so to speak. Wing dog?

"Come on, boy."

He snapped on a lead, even though Benji knew how to walk already, and followed the others heading to the front door. He nodded to a couple of kids, here with their mom and an ugly pug.

"Hey, aren't you Tom Chavez?" the boy asked.

He dipped the front of his snapback. "You like hockey?"

"Love it." The boy—Jarrett—started telling him about his peewee team, until his mom apologized for interrupting, and said they needed to get inside because the class was starting soon.

He agreed to Jarrett's request for a selfie, then held the door as they passed before him. Then kept it open as a couple of blondes smiled and said hello.

He nodded, but he was a brunette fan. More specifically, a Jessica James fan.

His heart tap-tapped a little faster as he followed the barking to a large room. Jess stood at the door, beside a couple of other women, welcoming them in. He couldn't help but notice her gaze was always on the dog first, then the person. He knew her well enough to recognize a sense of strain around her eyes, like she was feeling pressured, although she was trying to hide it with her smiles.

Sure enough, once the blondes had passed inside, her gaze fell on Benji. "Hello there. Aren't you gorgeous?"

If only she'd say that about him. Here went nothing, then. "Hey, Jess."

She looked up. Blinked. "Tom! What are you doing here?"

He tilted his head and smiled. "Isn't that obvious?"

Pink brushed her cheeks. "I didn't know you had a dog. Who's this?"

"Benji."

As if he'd heard his name, Benji sat and held out a paw, as if waiting for her to shake it.

She did so, then her blue-green gaze returned to him, filled with speculation, along with something else. "Are you sure you need training?"

"No. But I'm sure Benji can benefit from some pointers."

She laughed, and instantly that earlier sense of strain disappeared.

He smiled, and the rosy hue of her cheeks deepened. Dang, she was pretty.

"Okay, well it's your money."

"A solid investment." Especially if it meant she spent time talking to him.

She nodded, then one of the other helpers motioned to the person behind him, so he moved Benji to an unclaimed corner away from the blondes. He didn't need random women talking to him. Not when he was focused on one woman only.

Jarrett waved and he grinned back, then knelt beside Benji. Benji might never win one of the 'Pet dogs run along the ice' challenges posted by other teams, but he wasn't the kind to bark at butterflies either. While a number of the dogs seemed a little anxious here, Benji was calm, even-keeled, relaxed. Which basically meant he was a lot like his owner. Tom smirked at himself.

Jess clapped her hands, and instantly the noise calmed. "Good evening, and welcome to the first of our dog obedience classes. We're so glad you're here to learn how to teach your pet some basic commands." Her aqua eyes met his and he grinned.

Her gaze instantly veered away.

Okay, note to self: don't grin at the pretty instructor. Not when she's got a job to do.

The next hour passed in several instructions, then they were given plastic sandwich bags worth of dog treats to encourage their dog to obey. None of which Benji needed, something Jess seemed to cotton on to as she finally drew near.

"You were saving the best until last, huh?" He gestured to the others, some of whom were still struggling with a basic Sit command.

"I'm saving until last the dog and owner who clearly *don't* need training."

"Hey, I can't help it if Benji is a fast learner."

"So fast I suspect he'd learned it all before he came here today."

"Look, he's a smart dog. You can't hold that against him."

"No, but I can against you."

"Hey," he protested.

She smiled, and drew near. "But seriously," her smile faded a little. "It's good to see a friendly face. Today was kind of *ugh*."

He swallowed. Was this his chance to ask her out? Simply to let her blow off steam and share whatever had obviously bothered her about today, of course.

But before he could do so, a snarl-off between a kelpie and a mastiff had her racing away, employing her best stern teacher voice and tricks and bribes until the class soon closed.

He waited until the end, saluting Jarrett and his sister and mom, dipping his chin to the blondes, then waiting until an anxious-looking older lady and her little dachshund finished talking at her. Talking at, because the lady didn't seem to be giving much room for Jess to say anything.

Finally, she turned and saw him. "Tom, you're still here."

He moved closer. "Had to wait until your fans had all cleared."

"You're not a fan?"

Oh, he was president and number one ticket holder of the Jessica James fan club.

She seemed to realize what she'd said as she blushed again. "I meant—"

"All good." He scuffed a sneaker toe on the concrete floor. "I wanted to see if you're free to catch up. It's been a while."

She frowned. Oh. That didn't bode well. "You mean now?"

He shrugged. "I figured maybe you hadn't eaten yet, and it might be good to talk with a friend, especially if your day has been kind of"—how had she described it? Oh yeah—"ugh."

Her lips twisted, and she studied him a second then nodded. He internally fist-pumped. *Finally.* He would get a date with Jessie James.

"It's been a day, and I could use a friend. If you don't mind being used."

"Happy to be used any way you like."

She eyed him oddly.

"Uh, I mean in a strictly Christian and brotherly sense." Yeah, that wasn't what he meant either. He wanted a date—one day— with this lady. Not for her to think of him as a brother. Man. Why was this so much harder to say aloud than what he'd practiced in his head? "Um, so anyway, you tell me where you want to eat, and I'm your man."

Her gaze narrowed. "Just a meal?"

"Sure. Although I'm happy to do whatever you want." Like hold her hand. Or—

"I could do with food with a friend. Not a date."

"Uh, sure. I know that. We're just friends."

Just friends. He supposed it was better than nothing. But a shadow of what he really wanted.

Which was for Jessica James to see him as her knight in

shining armor, and for her to finally see what he'd long ago prayed about and concluded: that God had put them in this corner of the planet at the same time, because they were meant to be together.

He pushed back his shoulders. Good thing he was a patient man.

Two

"Hey, what does a duck like on a taco?" Tom asked.

Jess looked up from the filling spilling out the end of her taco. "What?"

"Guac."

Jess laughed, but still that core of tension thudded away, just as it had since that encounter with Giselle and poor Henrietta this afternoon. Dr. Theodore hadn't been pleased. In fact, he'd been downright disappointed when she finally got a chance to talk to him, saying she'd been unprofessional and overreacted. She'd longed to argue, but as he paid her wages she wasn't sure whether he would appreciate her objections. She'd longed to ask one of the other vets for their opinions, but it seemed they were all booked solid. At least the vet nurses seemed to be on her side, doing their best to calm poor Henrietta, and shaving her to release the worst of the dye.

She sighed, and instantly knew that was a mistake as Tom leaned forward. He seemed too interested, too eager to help. He couldn't actually like her or something, could he?

Please. She lowered her gaze. That was absurd. She wasn't the pretty sister. That was Poppy. Jess knew she was too plain-spoken and direct to ever be sweet enough to suit a man. And maybe her sisters had teased her about Tom's interest before, but it didn't mean anything could work out. Even if he was interested, she didn't have time to date, not if she wanted to pay off her student loans this century. So this was merely dinner, a catch up. A girl had to eat, after all.

"What's wrong?" His voice was low, his tone serious for once.

She shook her head. It was unprofessional to talk about the clinic's clients, wasn't it? Besides, Dr. Theodore had basically forbidden it. Although, from what Giselle had last been saying, she didn't seem the kind to keep mum about her problems with others—or blaming them. She sighed again.

"What's the matter?" Tom's hand crept across the table, touched her fingers.

She jerked, sending her taco remnants flying. "Oops. Sorry."

"My fault." He helped her pick up the mess, then signaled to a passing server for more napkins. "I'm sure Benji will help with the meat. That is, if Dr. Jess approves."

Oh, he was sweet. "Dr. Jess approves."

He picked up the meat and placed it in the metal bowl assigned to Benji, as this dog-friendly restaurant provided. Then glanced back at her. "Has a Dalmatian ever made you a taco?"

"No."

"They really hit the spot."

A chuckle escaped. "Are you going to give me taco jokes all night?"

"Why? Are they too cheesy?"

She mock-groaned even as she appreciated his attempt to lighten the mood.

He grinned, and her heart fluttered a little, just as it had when she'd seen him earlier. She broke the connection. This was a bad idea. He was Franklin's friend. She was too busy.

Her gaze lowered to patient Benji, definitely the best-behaved dog on this patio tonight. She gently rubbed him between his ears. "So, tell me about Benji. How long have you had him?"

Tom leaned back in his seat, his long legs stretching under the table, his sneakered foot nudging hers. "Sorry."

"It's okay. I'm used to Franklin taking up more than his fair share of space."

"Hey, I don't take up as much space as him," Tom protested.

No. Tom wasn't as tall or wide as Franklin—he'd probably never seen himself described as a Man Mountain the way Franklin had—but he sure took up more than his fair share of space in her brain. Which was dangerous. And exactly why she couldn't let that soft look in his eyes lead to anything more. Already a weird fluttery sensation in her chest proved she was strangely susceptible to this man's charm.

She had to steer this conversation back on track. "So, Benji?"

"I've had Benji a few weeks now." He rubbed his dog's head. "I got him from my sister when they couldn't keep him in their new apartment."

"I didn't know you had a sister."

"She's just moved to Regina. And yes, she did a good job training him."

"So you're looking after him or is he yours?"

"He's mine. I want to spend the summer getting him used to things."

"You're not going away? I know Franklin was talking about going to Europe with Hannah."

He shrugged. "I figured there's enough interesting things around here."

His gaze met hers again, and again she felt that shimmy of... *something* spark between them. She pressed her lips together.

He glanced at Benji. "Besides, I figured it wouldn't be fair to Benji to go place him somewhere else just because I might like a few days at the beach. Being a pet owner is a responsibility, right? It's about doing what's best for them, thinking of them, not just thinking of myself."

What a contrast to what she'd experienced with Giselle earlier.

A wave of emotion threatened her composure. She took a sip of her virgin margarita instead.

"Jess, I hope you don't mind me asking, but are you okay? You've seemed a little off today." He shifted closer, leaned his elbows on the table. "You mentioned before that your day was kind of rough."

Oh, he was kind. "I had to deal with someone who seems to hold the opposite opinion to you. She seemed to think her dog was there for her own amusement." There. Dr. Theodore couldn't object to that. Jess was simply offering her opinion, judgy as it might make her seem.

"I'm sorry. It must be hard to have to deal with situations where an animal suffers because of an owner's negligence."

His understanding wove beneath her defenses, stealing under her eyelids until she almost wanted to cry again. "That's it exactly."

His hand stole across the table, so she hurriedly patted Benji again. "You're such a good boy, aren't you?"

"Who just wants someone to love him."

Her attention jerked back to Tom. Had he meant that to sound flirty? Not that she spoke the language of flirt. But if she did, that would sound awfully close to what a flirty person might say. Right? Poppy would know. If only she'd thought to record this conversation, with all of its awkward stop starts, then maybe Poppy could best help her to interpret what was really going on.

Which was *nothing*, she told herself firmly. "This is not a date."

"I know."

Uh oh. Had she said that aloud? Biting her lip, she met his gaze. "I'm sorry. I'm a bit distracted. I've got so much going on in work, and I don't really think I have the time to do things like this."

"You mean to eat?"

"Well, yes. Of course I have to eat. But it's much quicker at home." Since giving up her apartment thanks to too-high rents and ungodly work hours that meant she was barely there, home often consisted of Franklin's spare room these days, when she wasn't able to spend weekends on the ranch. She didn't admit it to anyone, but she'd crashed more than a few nights at the clinic's infirmary, keeping an eye on the pets staying overnight. She'd even spent a couple of nights in her car, thanks to late nights and early starts. Sleeping in felt like a luxury she might never experience again. Her haphazard schedule meant meals usually consisted of something she could heat up in the microwave, which didn't help her budgeting any. So if she skipped the occasional meal to save some money, well, so be it.

His eyes softened. "I'm glad you could find time today."

"Well, like I said, it was good to see a friendly face."

"Especially when your day has been hard."

He paid attention. A little too well, perhaps. "It's been good to catch up, but I should probably go. I've got some studying to do."

His brow puckered. "I thought you'd finished all your studies."

"I have, but I've got some cases that require some more research, so, yeah." She reached for the bill.

His hand closed over hers, and again she felt that frisson of energy pulse between them. "It's okay. I've got this."

"But I can't let you pay for my meal. This is not a date," she reminded him.

"So you keep saying," he muttered. "Look, Jess, I asked if you want dinner. You're my friend, right? Well, I'm pretty sure I make more money than you, so it'd be rude for me to ask you to have dinner then make you pay. Sorry, I'm not that kind of guy."

She was half tempted to tell him not to be sorry. That she knew exactly what kind of guy he was. A good, kind, honorable man. But the kind of man who could so easily trip her up into wanting something she really couldn't afford to get involved with.

Instead, she settled on another truth. "Well, when you put it like that, then thank you. I appreciate it."

He grinned. "You can pay next time."

"Next time?"

"Jokes. I wouldn't ever expect a lady to pay. Call me old-fashioned, but there it is."

His smile made her heart see-saw again.

"But I'm not joking about there being a next time. I hope there will be, anyway." His green eyes shone with optimistic confidence.

"I..." How she hated to be the one to have to puncture this into reality. "I don't know if that's a good idea."

The sparkle faded. "Why not?"

"We're friends, Tom. You're Franklin's friend. I don't think he'd like to have us seeing each other."

"What business is it of his?"

"He's your teammate. And my brother. And, yeah, I'm not interested in dating anyone. Work is way too busy these days, I barely get enough sleep." Oops. Hadn't meant to spill that little nugget of truth. "So, thanks for this evening, but we probably shouldn't do this again."

He pressed his lips together, then nodded. "But we're still friends, right?"

"Friends," she agreed. Even if that hurt look in his eyes made her wonder if he wanted more. Which again felt ridiculous to even imagine. Why would a hot hockey player like him like her? She gathered her bag. Clearly she was tired. Her brain wasn't making sense.

"See you next week then," he murmured.

"Next week?"

"At obedience classes."

She snorted. "You don't need it."

"Hey, it never hurts to get some tips."

"Fine. It's your money." She scratched Benji's ears. "See you, Benji. You're a good boy." She grew aware of Tom's bare, tanned leg. Why had the man insisted on wearing shorts today that showed off his muscles? She backed away, glanced back at him, found a small smile. "See you, Tom."

"Take care, Jess. I, uh, I'll be praying for you."

Oh, why did he have to say that like that? Was he aware that his black hair made the green of his eyes pop? "Thanks." She knew the correct Christian thing to do would be to say she was praying for him too. But saying that invited an intimacy she wasn't sure she wanted. No, was *definitely* sure she didn't want. She couldn't afford to. She didn't want to. She wouldn't!

And to make sure she didn't fall from her all too fickle-feeling pledge, she'd tell Franklin what had happened tonight.

"You went on a date?" Franklin frowned. "With *Tom*?"

"Come on, Franklin. You heard her. They had dinner, that's all." Hannah sent Jess a sympathetic glance.

But Jess was pretty sure her sister-in-law, for all her smarts, hadn't cottoned on to the real state of affairs. How could she, when Jess barely knew it herself?

Yes, if she had a different job, one that didn't consume her every waking hour, then exploring something beyond friendship with Tom might be nice. *Would* be nice. He was a great guy. But as it was, work did consume every second of her life, so that was that.

"Look, he's a nice guy, but work is insane right now, so I really don't want to have to worry about anything else right now."

"Would you want to try for something with Tom if work was easier?" Hannah asked.

"Oh, look who is getting all in my face like Poppy and Cassie," Jess teased.

"Someone has to when they're not here."

Because Poppy was teaching at her friend Bailey's ballet school in Winnipeg, and Cassie was in California on a well-deserved mini-break, visiting her boyfriend, Harrison Woods, on the set of his new movie. She'd be back on the ranch next week when filming for the upcoming episodes of *As The Heart Draws* took over the ranch's western town for what might be its last season, now that Ainsley Beckett, its leading lady, had indicated she wanted out. Cassie had been so stressed upon hearing that, that she'd needed a time out.

"Do you want me to have a word with Tom?" Franklin asked.

Tom? Oh, right. "Look, I think I was pretty clear. You don't need to come down heavy on him. I'm probably misreading things anyway."

"Yeah, judging from what I've seen, you're not misreading things," Franklin said dryly.

Her heart skipped a beat or three. Okay, if *Franklin* of all people had noticed, then maybe she wasn't lost in some sad romantic fantasy of her own imagination. "He's a nice guy, but just not for me." Not while she kept this job, anyway.

Franklin nodded. "You won't need to worry about him."

"I'm not."

But from the determined look in her big brother's eye, maybe she now needed to be.

"...so I don't want you bothering her anymore, okay?"

Franklin's voice rattled through Tom's ear, echoing through the empty chasm within. It wasn't bad enough that he'd been friend-zoned by Jess. Now she'd gotten her brother to play the heavy and ensure it stayed that way.

"Message received." Loud and clear.

"Dude." Franklin sighed. "She's got a lot on her plate right now. Work is intense."

"I know. Which is why I thought she could do with a time-out. She's pretty stressed."

"You think I don't know that?" Franklin snapped.

Whoa. Someone hadn't taken his happy pills today. "You okay, Franklin?"

"I'm fine. I'm just annoyed that one of my friends has gone behind my back and is trying to date my sister without asking me first."

He took a deep breath and tried to sound as reasonable as he could. "Why would I have to ask you? Are you saying I need your permission?"

"Don't put words in my mouth. It's just a respect thing."

"Well, respectfully, I like your sister, but I really feel like it's between me and her. And I respect her so I won't ask her out on a date again. Okay?" Not until she gave some kind of sign it would be welcome, anyway.

"You promise?"

"Man. What do you take me for? Come on."

Now he thought about it, he didn't think that Jess would ask her brother to step in. She'd made her position clear. This sounded more like Franklin himself had decided to play the heavy. Which made him wonder why he didn't trust him.

"Have I done something wrong?" he asked. "Is there a reason you don't trust me? I would've thought you'd like your sister to date a guy you know."

"Thought I knew," Franklin muttered.

"You still know me. Man, I'm part of a Bible study group with you. Why are you getting upset?"

"I'm not upset. But I don't want my sister upset, either."

"*Is* she upset?" he asked quickly. If she was, he'd back right off, and not attend another dog training night. Even if not seeing her all summer killed him.

"No," Franklin admitted. "I just want her to stay that way. She's stressed enough with all the work she has to do."

Whereas Tom was fairly sure Jess could do with something to take her mind off work, to relax, to laugh. He'd happily offer himself as tribute for all three.

He cleared his throat. "I appreciate the phone call, and your concern. But you do not need to worry about me. We're friends, that's all. I care about her, and I'll do whatever I can to make life easier for her, so you don't need to worry about me. Okay?" *Lord, change his heart. Whatever is bothering him, make him see sense so it stops.*

"Fine." Franklin blew out a breath. "Hannah and I are going to Italy in a few weeks."

He appreciated the change in topic. "That'll be nice for you both."

Franklin mentioned a few highlights of where they'd go, and by the time the call finished Tom felt like their friendship had strayed back into something approaching normality, after the rocky few moments earlier. *Thanks, God.*

But it only doubled his prayers for Jess. If Franklin was worried about the amount of hours his sister was working, then there had to be something to worry about. Hannah worked long hours, and had experienced more than her share of workplace bullying and harassment. Franklin had stepped in and helped there, so Tom knew Franklin was the over-protective type.

But if he was concerned about Jess that likely meant there was something to be concerned about. Which meant Tom would do what he could to be the friend she needed. Even if she might not wish him to be around much at all.

THREE

nother week passed with long hours and challenging
situations. While it was good to see Henrietta had
improved, her owner's reaction had not helped matters.

"See?" Giselle had said. "It wasn't as bad as you said. I knew
this was an overreaction."

Jess had received the impression that Dr. Theodore agreed. It
hadn't helped when Giselle had posted to her thousands of
followers that her precious pet had been dognapped. The vet
clinic had received hate mail on their socials, which Dr. Theodore
had laid firmly at her feet.

"How many times did I tell you to be careful with this client?
Giselle has the opportunity to make or break businesses. Why did
I ever send you?"

An excellent question. The only silver lining was this debacle
might've disqualified her from being sent out like that again.

But the drama with Henrietta wasn't the only one. The past
week had seen several cases where she'd needed to advise people to
put their animals down, which was always so hard. Not just on
the pet owners, but on veterinarians too. She'd come into this
business to save lives, not end them. But sometimes the most

humane thing was to put an animal out of its suffering, even if its owners couldn't understand or see the seriousness of their conditions. But sometimes cancer or liver or brain issues weren't always apparent until too late.

Then there was the tightrope of balancing budgets and expectations, both hers and the owners. Why was it that so often the rich were prepared to treat their pets carelessly or dump them or refuse to pay their bills, while those who desperately loved their pets couldn't afford to pay? People didn't realize that increased pet ownership combined with decreased staff equaled decreased staff ratios and increased stress. Studies showed that the amount of veterinarian graduates only just kept pace with retirements, and weren't meeting the ever increasing gap in pet ownership.

Coupled with this was a huge gap in vet nurses which only added to the stress and increased bills due to higher wages needed to retain them. Increased costs only led to more abandoned pets, which all combined for a vicious cycle of stress.

Something of this was hinted in the voice mail from the phone call she'd missed from Lisette, the only other female and valedictorian of their class. Lisette had also found employment at a big city clinic, and her request for Jess to call her back still remained unanswered. So much to do. So many obligations. So much worry about how to juggle it all. So much stress.

Stress, that pounded away in her head, behind her eyes, that appeared on her skin by way of eczema. Stress, that made her snap, that made her temper short, her patience thin. Her days were filled with trouble, and it seemed a rare appointment when it was a simple kennel cough injection. She looked forward to those with acute longing. At least she'd get out to the ranch for Father's Day soon, and have time to see Belle, her horse, and Buster, her terrier. It had been way too long since she'd seen her two favorite animals.

Thank goodness for those moments to pop her head above water. And for times like tonight's dog training. Although she hoped last week's conversation with Tom wouldn't make things awkward.

Her headache, already in play, doubled at the sound of the dogs yapping in the room. She'd let Denise, her assistant, do the welcoming tonight, so she had a moment to snatch a bite—a protein bar—so she'd have an excuse in case Tom asked her for another meal. Even if Mexican with him had been the best meal she'd eaten in weeks.

She paused at the door. Peered inside. Where—? Oh, there. She winced. Front row. It'd be hard to avoid him tonight. *Lord, give me strength.*

She entered the room, waving at those who had returned. It seemed they were only missing a couple of people from last time, which didn't matter too much, considering they'd all paid upfront.

"Good evening, everyone." She clapped to get their attention from her position in the front. Directly in front of Tom. Had he placed himself there deliberately? "Hello, everyone. Welcome to another week of dog obedience training. Great to see you all back. How did you do last week?"

A few people commented, Tom wasn't one of them. She wasn't willing to look at him yet.

"So today we're going to practice walking on a leash."

Tom snickered.

Her cheeks heated. "Practice walking our dogs on a leash," she quickly corrected. "And for that I'm going to use Sylvester here," the anxious older lady's dachshund, "to be our demonstrator, if that's alright with you, Margaret."

"Oh, that'd be wonderful if she can practice with you. I'm afraid my legs are so tired, and—"

"Thanks, Margaret." It felt rude to cut her off, but the class didn't have time to listen. The dogs certainly didn't. "So, when you're walking your dog, you want your dog to make sure they are keeping pace with you. Not walking ahead, definitely not dragging you, but also sometimes you'll need to encourage them to come along."

One of the blonde women she'd seen checking out Tom last week put up her hand. "Does the length of the dog's legs make a difference?"

"Well, yes. A Great Dane is going to need a much longer stride than a dachshund or pug. And the fitness of the animal affects your walk too. We definitely don't want to be dragging our dog along."

Tom put up his hand.

"Yes, Tom?"

"Why did the boy name his dog Five Miles?"

"Why?"

"So he could tell his gym teacher he walked Five Miles every day."

Her lips twitched, as the room filled with groans and some laughter. "Thank you. Now, perhaps we can all practice holding our leashes like so," she demonstrated, "and I'm going to ask you to follow me in a line around the markers." She pointed to the orange plastic cones anchoring the room's corners. "In single file, let's go."

She gestured for Margaret to accompany her, and showed her the correct length of leash to hold the dog. Tom, she noted, had fallen in directly behind her, and she couldn't help but notice how perfectly Benji was doing this. Especially as most of the other dogs were not.

Margaret complained about her knees, her hips, her attention seemingly more on her personal health than what Jess was trying to teach her. Honestly, what was the point in doing classes if people didn't pay attention? She bit back a sigh.

"Hey Margaret," Tom called. "Why is a Dachshund a good dog to have?"

She peered back at him. "Why?"

"Because they're all *wieners*."

Margaret chuckled, and Jess swallowed a smile. She turned back to him. "Have you memorized dog jokes?"

"No." He grinned. "Well, maybe a few. What's a magician's favorite dog breed?"

She didn't want to ask. She really didn't. But something about his charm made her weaken. "What?"

"The labracadabrador."

She laughed, and shook her head, then gave the leash to Margaret. She couldn't do her job if he kept this up. "Keep going Margaret, you're doing fine."

"How am I doing?" Tom asked.

"You obviously need to be kept on a tight leash."

He chuckled, the husky burble warming her heart. How long since she'd made a guy laugh? But no. She couldn't be distracted by him, so she went to the next person. One of the blondes. She subtly checked out her name on the sticker nametag. "Hey Maddison, how are you and Fluffy doing?"

Maddison seemed to be having some trouble with her chihuahua. Which might be because she was checking out the muscled legs of the man in front of her. Tom really shouldn't be distracting the ladies by wearing shorts. It wasn't fair.

"Hey Margaret, how does a Japanese Chihuahua say hello?"

Jess smiled. He was at it again.

"I don't know, Tom."

"Konichihuahua."

"Tom, stop," Jess protested, as Maddison collapsed into giggles.

He peered over his shoulder. "Sorry, were you eavesdropping?"

She glanced away, refocusing on correcting Maddison's leash-holding technique. "See how that's easier?"

She made her way around the others, realizing that some dogs —Benji, for sure—had much better skills, and were feeling stifled by the shuffle of the dog in front.

By the time she finished inspecting people's walking techniques, she could tell some of the dogs—and people—needed a drink. "Let's take a drink break for two minutes then rejoin."

She had to deal with several questions from some others, so it was closer to five minutes before she finally could restore order. She clapped for their attention. "Walking the dog is something I want you all to practice over the upcoming days. We'll return to it again in our next lesson. Now, let's return to our sitting—teaching our dogs to sit, I mean, in case that's confusing for anyone." She eyed Tom then glanced away. "Let's see how that's been going."

She made her rounds, plied her treats, and did her best to ignore Tom's jokes. But somehow they kept drifting to her ears.

"Why aren't Corgi jokes funny? Because they're really short."

"Yesterday I spotted an albino Dalmatian. It was the least I could do for it."

"Why are dogs terrible dancers? Because they have two left feet."

"Why do dogs tend to run in circles? Because it's really hard to run in squares."

She bit back her smiles. *Ignore him, ignore him.* He might be making the evening more enjoyable, and definitely added much needed lightness to her day, but she couldn't afford to be distracted. *Wouldn't* be distracted.

Which was all well and good until she got to the end, and again he was waiting to talk to her, having already helped Denise pack up the equipment. She tensed. She didn't want any more awkwardness. Franklin, she suspected, had only made things more embarrassing for them. She gestured for him to walk with her down the hall to the clinic's entrance.

"Good lesson today."

"Thanks. Although I think we'll have a larger dog, like Benji leading that kind of exercise next week."

Tom smirked. "Leading, exercise. I see what you did there."

She internally groaned. What was the man doing to her? His dumb dog jokes were infecting her brain! But he had also added a much-needed fun factor. Even Denise and the other helper had said the same.

"How has your week been?" he asked.

"More of the usual. Busy. Stressful. You know."

"I'm on vacation right now, but yeah, I know how it can be."

His playing season that saw weeks of travel interspersed with pockets of time at home.

"Hey, how are things after the Henrietta mess?"

She winced. "You saw that?"

"Giselle has a big mouth and some skills with social media. I don't normally read that stuff, but I put two and two together."

"The main thing is that the dog is fine. She's no longer pink, and Giselle might not have appreciated all of the comments her posts have received. Apparently I'm not the only one who gets upset when animals' lives are put at risk thanks to someone's vanity and pride."

"You did the right thing," he assured.

"Thanks." She needed to remember that.

Silence stretched between them, as the specter of last week loomed. *What to say, what to say...*

Benji pushed his head to her leg, and she leaned down and patted him. "Can I give him a treat?"

"Of course."

She gave Benji one of her spare treats, and rubbed his head, gently tugging at his ears.

Tom cleared his throat. "Your big brother threatened me."

She winced. Peered up. "I'm so sorry. I didn't ask him to."

"I figured that. You were pretty clear."

Discomfort rippled across her. "I hope I didn't sound mean. You're a nice guy—"

He rolled his eyes. "Just what every guy likes to hear."

"—and I appreciate that I can be real with you. So thank you."

He shook his head. "Think nothing of it. I'm trying not to."

Huh?

"Hey Jessie, you have a phone call," Denise called, holding the after hours phone.

She exhaled, the momentary respite of the night's jokes dissipating as the pressure ramped up again. "Sorry, I've got to go. I'm on the emergency shift."

His brow knit. "You seem to do that quite often."

Was he keeping tabs on her? "Someone's got to." And the junior vet was cheaper to pay overtime than the more experienced ones. "I've got to take this."

"Praying for you, Jess."

She bit a suddenly trembling lip. "Thanks," she whispered. Then gave Benji a hurried pat, and exited.

TOM WATCHED HER GO, the sudden shimmer to her eyes and slump to her shoulders as she hastened out the door reigniting his concerns. He'd wondered about the wisdom of returning tonight, especially after the shut out she'd given him following last week's non-date. But the weariness he'd seen in her that he hoped his dumb jokes had alleviated a little—he thought he'd seen her smile —made him think coming again tonight hadn't been a bad idea after all.

"Come on Benji." He clicked and Benji followed him out to his vehicle.

After strapping him in, he got inside and sat, his own shoulders slumping. What to do... what to do... He could go home, but his condo felt a little lonely. He could visit a teammate—he bet Mike and Bree Vaughan would gladly welcome him in, but he didn't want to see a picture of domestic bliss and be reminded of what he didn't have. Franklin was an obvious no-go zone. Not yet, anyway. A little more water would need to pass under that bridge before things felt mended. He hoped that Franklin and Hannah's time in Italy would help the man relax.

It was a shame his parents lived in Saskatchewan otherwise

he'd call in there. The night felt too young to go home. Watching TV felt lame. And a book was good but sometimes he just needed people interaction. He could jump on the Bible study online chat and see if anyone was free to talk, but even that felt like he might be goading Franklin, so he wouldn't do that.

Benji woofed, the sound reminding him that he hadn't eaten, and neither had Benji. He'd half wondered about seeing if Jess needed to eat, but her working after hours suggested she couldn't.

But wait. Maybe that was the answer. She obviously would need to eat, so he could get her some food and drop it off. He didn't need to eat with her, but she'd surely appreciate it. Maybe even appreciate the thought that went with it, and some day appreciate him—

No. That was selfish. He'd simply bless her with a meal. No strings attached. Even if she didn't want to eat with him ever again.

He returned to the Mexican place from last week and ordered what they'd gotten last week. This time he split the tacos, giving her some of his beef while he took one of her chicken tacos. Once they were split between two takeout bags, he returned to the vet clinic.

The lights were on, and a fierce yowling from the back suggested Jess had her hands full. He deposited the bag on the front counter, wrote her name on it with a black marker, and left, praying for her.

He was halfway home when his phone rang, and he answered through the car's audio system. Michelle. "Hey sis."

"Tom, are you driving?"

At the sound of her voice Benji started barking.

"Aw, is that my puppy I can hear?" she crooned.

"Nope. It's *my* puppy you can hear."

"You know he's a loaner."

"I know no such thing. I seem to remember that you gave him to me fair and square."

She sighed. "Yes, we did. But I still miss him. How is he doing?"

"He's enjoying Mexican."

"What? You're not feeding him Mexican, are you?"

"Hey, the vet said that's okay, so I'm going with her advice."

"Her, huh?"

Darn. He'd always been a little careful about his love life with his family. His sister and mom were way too inclined to read things that simply weren't there.

"Who is she?"

His sister was like a dog with a bone. "She's the sister of a teammate."

She gasped. "Not Franklin James's sister?"

"You know this how?"

"Someone snapped a picture of you the other day with a woman and posted it on the hot hockey hero site and a friend sent the link to me. Someone commented and said she thought she looked like Jess someone. You were at a Tex-Mex restaurant or something."

"Man."

"So it's true?"

"We were eating together. It was *not* a date." He exhaled.

"Oh, but judging from that sigh you'd like it to be."

He hated how his sister had always had this uncanny insight into his life. "She's super stressed at the moment and doesn't have time for a relationship, so it's not the right time apparently."

"Oh, baby bro, that sucks."

"Yes it does." But indulge in a pity party he would not. "So, how's Travis?"

"He's busy climbing the corporate ladder. Good thing I have Sadie to keep me company."

Their baby daughter, just six weeks old. "We could come on a road trip to visit you."

"You'd do that?" Her voice held hope.

"It's got to beat hanging around here." Feeling lonely.

Wishing for a certain vet to finally see him as more than a friend. It didn't seem like her job would be easing up any time soon.

In fact, the more he thought about it, the more it sounded like an excellent idea. "We could make a couple of weeks of it. Maybe catch up with Mom and Dad too." They'd be sure to want to see him, their favorite son. Their only son.

"You don't have any commitments?"

"Nothing important." The dog training lessons were prepaid, and he really didn't need to take Benji to them. It was obvious to all. Even Margaret and Blonde One and Blonde Two had said how good Benji was at everything. He could skip the lessons. Jess probably wouldn't even miss him.

"Well, let me check with Travis and Mum and Dad, but that'd be awesome. Maybe we could get a cabin by the lake like in the olden days."

At the mention of olden days his mind tripped to the western town perched in the middle of the Three Creek Ranch spread Franklin and Jessica's parents owned. There were rustic cabins among the historical storefronts used in TV shows like *As The Heart Draws* that could be rented. And as tempting as it was to suggest they hire one of those, he figured Jess—and definitely Franklin—would probably like a break from him.

"You probably should check with Travis and find out his schedule first."

"Good thinking. But it'd be so good if we could stay like we used to, even hang around together for Canada Day."

"I don't know how much availability there'd be at this late stage," he warned.

"Well, money talks, and you've got some."

True, even if his pay was hardly at the grade of the team's superstars.

His sister sighed. "It'd be awesome to see you again, Tom."

"And Benji. I know he's the real drawcard here."

"Absolutely," she teased.

He smiled. Well, maybe he couldn't have the woman of his

dreams—not yet, anyway—but God had blessed him with a family he loved, which he knew in this world was an increasing rarity. And maybe, with the people who knew him best, he might be able to get some clues about how to help the woman who had secured his heart to see him as more than just a friend.

FOUR

"I'm afraid we're going to have to reschedule things," Dr. Theodore said the next week.

"I beg your pardon?"

"Jess, we need you to work this Sunday after all."

"But it's Father's Day. I'd made plans."

"I'm afraid you're going to have to unmake them." Dr. Theo's face was impassive.

"But all my family will be there." A rare thing. "And they have to travel back on Monday." Franklin and Hannah were only staying on Sunday because it was Father's Day, then on Monday they'd fly to Rome. And while she got to see them regularly, it wasn't the same as when they were all together.

"It's the way it's always been. We have to work together as a team, Jessie."

Except it seemed she was the one always doing the heavy lifting. She tamped down those words with effort. "I have a rostered day off on Monday. Dr. Theodore, I really need to have some time out. I'm exhausted."

"You'll get used to the hours."

"But I'm not sure I will. It's been constant overtime for

months now. And I know I'm new, but this almost feels over-whelming."

"Are you saying you're not up to the job?"

If she said yes, would he fire her? "Of course I can do it."

"Good. We'll need you on call on Sunday."

But that wasn't what she meant. "But sir—"

The look he sent her made her swallow the rest of her protest.

Then, as he walked away, she sank in her desk chair, the computer screen a blur. She pushed her head in her hands. This didn't seem fair. Her contract she was sure had stipulated she was to do no more than a certain number of hours overtime per week, and already she'd done ten. Was she being taken advantage of? It sure felt like it. "God, what do I do?"

A throbbing began behind her right eye, and she groaned. Popped two pain meds. She needed a clear head. Steady hands. She needed sleep. She needed *sleep*!

But when was she going to sleep considering her life was one big rush, rush, rush?

She still hadn't had time to return Lisette's call, her life too full of procedures, policies, dealing with clients, writing up notes. She hadn't seen her folks, her dog, her horse for what felt like years! Mom had tried to call recently, and now she'd have to say she couldn't make it, after all. She gritted her teeth. It seemed so unfair.

Even tonight, she had an online training meeting, then tomorrow would be the dog obedience class. At least that might provide some lightness.

Tom was a light-bringer in her world. A life bringer, too. A blessing bringer. After last week's class, when she'd had to rush to attend a cat that had been caught in barbed wire, she'd finally, wearily, returned to the front desk and noticed the bag of tacos with her name written on it. That had to have been Tom. A quick rewind of the security video showed it was. He continued to be thoughtful. She wondered what he'd do tomorrow, if he'd learned any new jokes. She hated to admit it, but a tiny part of her was looking forward to seeing him.

She plunged her head in her hands. "But it doesn't mean anything, Lord. You know it can't." As the busyness of her work continued to prove.

He wasn't here.

She pushed to her toes and glanced around tonight's dog class attendees and no. He wasn't here. Her heart dipped in a rush of disappointment.

"Where's Tom?" Margaret asked.

"I don't know."

"I thought you two were friends."

She shrugged. "I'm not his keeper."

"Maybe he's got a date."

Her heart tripped. Maddison, one of the blondes was missing tonight. Had he gone out with her? "Or maybe he's just unwell." *Lord, let him be okay. And Benji too.*

If something was really wrong, Franklin would've told her. Wouldn't he? Unless he didn't think she should know.

"He's an adult. He's entitled not to come." Especially as he'd already paid.

For a moment she wondered about Dr. Theo's percentage of her dog training fees. Surely her bank balance should reflect the extra hours she was doing with the dog training. Yet it hadn't seemed to have changed much at all, the pay much the same. Which was great. Greatly awkward. How could she find out if she was being ripped off? It was hardly the kind of thing one could ask a boss easily. Still, it was something else she needed to chase up, along with all the other things. Pressure ramped up. He didn't seem to appreciate her asking so many questions.

She checked on the participants' dog sitting and dog walking techniques, then led them into the trickier food commands. And grew acutely aware what a difference Tom's presence and jokes made to the evening. This felt far more clinical, methodical, going through the motions. Or maybe that was the sense of drudgery she felt, like this was another chore.

Who could she talk to about whether she was being ripped off? The rest of the staff seemed very loyal to Dr. Theo, and the other vets weren't exactly the confiding types. They seemed to have perfected the art of treating this as a job more than a vocation, their dispassionate natures almost robotic at times. Show up, do their jobs, offload what they could to the new girl—Jess—then go home to their families. Maybe she'd call Lisette tonight after this. She'd felt an increasing desire to call her.

But when she finally was released, she was so tired she didn't think it was safe to drive to Franklin's. So she got her sleeping bag from the back, grabbed the pillow from the backseat, and had a quick snooze. Then she'd be alert enough to safely drive to Franklin's.

A quick snooze that was only broken by the tapping on the window in the morning, when Dr. Theo frowned at her, gesturing for her to wind the window down.

"What? Huh?" Her hair was mussed, her eyes bleary. Turned out sleeping in her car in the clinic's yard wasn't as quiet as she'd hoped it would be. A drunk-looking beggar had stumbled through, clattering a garbage can lid and startling her awake. It'd taken ages to return to sleep. It took her a moment to recall she had to turn the car on to access the power for the accessories. She turned it on, powered down the window. "Morning."

"Did you sleep here?"

She yawned. Realized she *really* needed to brush her teeth. Gross. "I, uh, was pretty tired last night and meant to have a nap before driving home, but it turns out my nap went longer than I thought."

He peered at her. "Is that a sleeping bag? Why do you have one of those?"

"Because..." How to explain she'd used it several times before, when he'd rostered her on overnight shifts. "It's handy?"

"If this is too much for you, then say the word and we'll find a replacement."

Did he mean it? *Oh, thank You God.* This was an answer to prayer! "Well, sir, it *is* a lot. And like I said, I've been doing a lot of overtime, so if you could please find someone else to do the shift this Sunday that'd be awesome."

He frowned. "I didn't mean we'd replace you this Sunday. No, no, that must go ahead. Unless of course you don't feel like you have it in you to be a real veterinarian like we employ here at Ramesky Veterinary Clinic."

Wait—he was threatening to replace her? "You want to fire me?"

"If this kind of behavior continues, you may leave us with no other choice."

"But sir, I'm doing all that you're asking. I'm going above and beyond."

He sniffed. "Hardly that, I'm afraid."

"What more can I do?"

"Well, you could stop complaining about things, that'd make a nice start."

"When have I complained?"

"Saying you've got all these extra shifts, like you're the first person who has ever had to work overtime. I don't know what has come to this generation. I think they call your generation snowflakes, don't they?"

Her jaw sagged. Should she be offended, or shut up, seeing this man pulled the strings to her employment?

"Sir, I—"

"No, I'm prepared to overlook this today, seeing as you're obviously not used to hard work. But I expect you to make a real effort from now on. Understand?"

She nodded, her eyes filling with foolish tears. People might call her Jessie James, thinking she was always a straight shooter, but they didn't see these moments, when she felt powerless and weak. Never had she thought trying to help animals would make her feel like she was trapped within a cage.

"ARE you sure you can't come?" Poppy pleaded.

Jess studied the phone video, forcing a smile. "I really wish I could. You've got no idea how much." For all Dr. Theo's warnings about the need for a vet on the premises, they hadn't had a peep to justify her being on call. Yet traveling to the ranch, an hour away, was too far in case a real emergency occurred. Hence she was stuck here. Wishing. Hoping. Praying. Watching the others eat and laugh and enjoy while she was stuck here.

"It sounds like your boss is a tyrant," Poppy said.

The best answer to that was none.

"I'm sure he can't be that bad," her mom said.

Nothing to be too sure of there. Behind her mom, she saw how Franklin and Hannah glanced at each other. They thought that too? Why hadn't they said anything? Disgruntlement at the humans in her life made her long for a non-human companion. "Hey, can someone please put Buster on?"

Cassie held up Buster, complete with his ragamuffin hair. "Here he is."

"Hi sweetie," Jess called. Then frowned. "He seems a little lethargic."

"He's been off his food lately," her mom called.

"And you didn't tell me?"

"I'm sorry, hon. I meant to mention it the other night when you called to say you couldn't come, and I'm afraid I quite forgot."

Concern twisted her insides. Waiting here was dumb. She should be with her family. On Father's Day, no less. Sure, Dad didn't make a fuss about these things, but she wanted—needed—to be with them. Needed to feel their hugs, their love. To feel like she was okay in the world. To make sure that Buster was okay, too.

"I'm going to come."

"You are?" Mom's brow puckered. "Are you sure?"

"Nobody's called. It's been dead in here."

"I hope not literally," Harrison said. He'd returned with Cassie from California, in time for the shooting of the new series tomorrow.

"Not today." The animals that were here could all survive without her for a few hours. She'd go, get some life-saving hugs, eat some food, then return, and nobody would be any the wiser. A solid plan. "I'll see you all soon."

"Yay!" Poppy called. "I need you here so we can tease Cassie and Harrison about wedding dates."

"Poppy!" Cassie's jaw gaped.

More disconcerting feelings swept across her. "You're engaged?" Why hadn't she told her? Her eyes filled. Man, she was tired.

"We're not engaged," Cassie said firmly. "Poppy just wishes she had someone in her life."

"Clearly." Poppy's dry tone and rolled eyes said otherwise.

"We'll see you soon, honey." Her mom smiled.

"Can't wait. Love you, Dad!" she called.

"Love you, too, Jessie," he said at last. Typical Dad, waiting until the others had spoken.

She ended the call, excitement filling her chest. For the first time in a long time she finally had some sense of control back in her life. Control to make decisions about what she did and when. Not just be at the beck and call of a despot of a boss. Poppy was right, Dr. Theo was a tyrant. He seemed to pick on her. Why hadn't she ever realized this?

She checked the animals one more time, and grabbed the emergency phone just in case. If someone did call, then she could be back within the hour, otherwise she could advise they try another clinic. Theirs wasn't the only one in the city that might be open. And if by some chance Dr. Theo happened to call by—highly unlikely, because he was off enjoying his Father's Day with his family, wasn't he?—then she could always say she was on an emergency visit just outside the city limits. An emergency visit to see her family and animals, because if she didn't see them soon she might just lose her mind. That sounded like an emergency enough to her.

So there. It was settled. She'd go.

She locked up and got in her Nissan, and began the drive, pushing the speed limit the whole way. It was like her car knew how important this was to her, urging her to get there.

She'd just reached the city limits when the phone rang. The vet clinic's emergency phone. She bit back a word and looked for a spot to pull over. But the lumber trucks didn't let her move over. Panic rose, and although she knew it was wrong, she stabbed the green button to answer. "Hello?"

"Finally! Is this the vet? I have a sick cat that keeps vomiting and I don't know what to do."

Her heart fell, and she was sorely tempted to tell the man to try someplace else. But that wasn't fair. They would have someone who'd need to be called in too. Possibly someone who was a father. That wasn't fair, just because she wanted to play hooky.

"I'll see you shortly," she muttered, then ended the call.

Then looked for a place to turn around, which was hard to do, when her eyes were blinded with tears.

"Oh, this is so nice, isn't it?"

Tom glanced across to where his sister sat on a Muskoka chair, her feet up, drink in hand, the worries of new motherhood far away as she relaxed, knowing there were four other adults eager to help with little Sadie. Well, he was more willing than actually eager, and he suspected Dad was, too. But he'd seen the stress Michelle had been under, and a miracle of a reservation cancellation—or maybe Travis had known he'd needed to pull a few strings for the sake of his marriage—had seen this spot on Lake Waskesiu pop up, which he'd secured as soon as possible.

"Sure is peaceful."

And while it was peaceful and nice, and he'd loved seeing how Benji and Michelle had reconnected, and the curiosity then care Benji had displayed around little Sadie, sprawled on her back on the baby blanket, he couldn't help but feel a sense of disconnect, too. To wonder whether he'd ever get the chance to be a dad, to celebrate Father's Day like his own had, with a brand new joke book from Tom that he'd loved and instantly produced some groaners. He might be in his late twenties, but he'd rather be a young dad, one like Mike Vaughan, his team captain, who had juggled the responsibilities of fatherhood with hockey really well, even when life had had its challenging moments in recent years. Better to be young than too old and unable to run around like some of the dads he'd seen here.

Here, he was the odd man out. The one assigned to the room with bunk beds, like he was a kid. And he couldn't help wishing that he had a wife and was entitled to a room with her. Even if that one-day wife might be stuck with him in a room with bunk beds. They could have fun making it work. And even if the woman he wanted for a wife might be so career-focused she wouldn't want kids for years. He could cope with that, too.

He exhaled, studying the remains of the ice cubes swirling in the bottom of his diet cola. How was she? He hoped she'd gotten a break this weekend.

"What's that sound for?" Michelle asked, poking him with a talon she liked to call a fingernail. How she changed diapers with those things was beyond him.

"Nothing."

"Something."

"Yes, Tom, honey, are you okay?" his mom asked.

"It's that girl, isn't it?" Michelle said.

"Nope."

"Uh uh. You know lying is a sin."

"So is exasperating your brother."

"Yeah, I don't recall seeing that one in the Bible."

"What are you exasperated about, Son?" his dad asked.

"He met a girl, and she doesn't love him back," Michelle sing-songed.

"You're in love?" his mom yelped. "Aw, sweetie."

How had it escalated to this? "Mom, no."

"No?"

Well, that might actually be a lie. But saying it out loud to his family was a bit much when he'd never really contemplated it as being anything more than having *very strong feelings* for Jess. So no, it wasn't love. Yet. "No. I like her, that's all."

"And she turned you down?"

"Who is she?" Travis asked.

"Someone I met through work."

"Franklin James's sister," Michelle said helpfully. "I told you that already."

Great. Good to know his family was gossiping about him. He slouched in his chair as the summer sun beat down, and a couple of powerboats howled their way across the lake sending wake-waves to the shore.

"Hey, Son, what happened to the two vampires who went on their date?"

"What, Dad?" He knew what to say, even though he was pretty sure he knew the answer.

"It was love at first bite."

"Ha ha."

"You like that? What about this one: why should you never laugh at your significant other's choices?"

"Why?"

"Because you happen to be one of them."

As his dad chuckled, Tom found a smile, before rolling his eyes at his sister.

"Hey, did you hear the one about the two antennas who met on a roof?"

"Let me guess: they had a strong connection."

"You got it!" His dad's drink sloshed from the glass as he slapped his knee.

"I wonder if you'll ever be as bad as these two." Michelle poked Travis.

"I hope not," he muttered, drawing Tom's reluctant smile.

So a lifetime of corny joke-telling had rubbed off on him. He preferred to think it made him fun, rather than too serious like so many people in the world. The world needed more laughter, not more stress.

His smile faded as his thoughts returned to Jess again. She needed more laughter in her world, and definitely not more stress. He wondered how she was doing, whether she'd noticed he hadn't been at the dog training three days ago, whether she'd missed him, even a little bit. Was it bad to hope she had? Then he stopped wondering, and started praying for her. That God would sustain her, help her to have a fun day with her dad and family. And pray that one day she'd find the man who could help balance her life so she could find the peace and joy she desperately needed.

Bless her Lord. He slouched deeper in his seat, resting a hand on Benji's head, who seemed to sense his inner turmoil and pushed his head into Tom's palm.

And, God, I pray You'd bring along her right guy soon.

He swallowed the boulder-sized lump in his throat. This next bit required real faith.

Even if that guy's not me.

FIVE

nother week passed, and then another without Tom at dog training. The one bright spot in her week, snuffed out. Had he really taken her so seriously and thought she didn't want to see him again? It was getting harder to believe he was just busy. Franklin was in Italy, so she couldn't ask him. Wouldn't, anyway, because that would just invite unnecessary questions. But Tom seemed to have fallen off the planet.

She didn't like social media much, but she'd used the clinic's Instagram account to see if he'd posted anything on Insta. He hadn't, except for a shot on Father's Day that showed him smiling with his family. The selfie with his shirt unbuttoned had scored a number of comments. She read every last one of them.

Ugh—was that Maddison? The blonde from dog training? Maybe it was true and the two of them were dating. If so, kudos to Maddison for that seemed like fast work. But then some women seemed to know how to work it, to flaunt their femininity and capture a guy's attention, while she had always felt a little fake trying to act in some way not like herself. And seeing she was such a mess these days, overworked, overburdened and overwhelmed, it was probably good she'd never tried to have some fake persona to maintain. She couldn't do fake when she could barely handle reality.

Friday morning came, and with it, the usual cacophony of tasks demanding attention. Neutering cats. Dealing with worms. Another dog that had parasites. A dumped cat with kittens needing homes. So much need, so much suffering, so many desperate people with desperate situations. People who couldn't pay. People who argued because they didn't understand why the costs had increased. She was the whipping post for their verbal lashes.

Dr. Theo didn't like her. The other vets ignored her. She wanted—needed—help, but nobody seemed to notice. She was slowly sinking, drowning in a sea of responsibility.

Even her quick visit home recently had raised concerns. Buster wasn't eating, and all her knowledge wasn't helping. What kind of vet did that make her if she couldn't even help her own pet? A bad one, that's what. A selfish one, that's who. One who couldn't cope with the work or the responsibilities—she who had prided herself on her smarts and work ethic all her life! Obviously she wasn't nearly as smart as her family believed.

As she waited for Paige to arrive with the kitten needing castration she scratched at the eczema on her hands, the itch on her skin a perpetual buzz of annoyance, just like the weight of responsibilities she was drowning in, that nobody seemed to notice. She wished Tom was here. He might notice. Would he notice if she commented on his Instagram post? She rarely used her Instagram, never posting anything. But no, she couldn't do that. Could she? Did friends do that? Or would he think she was weird?

Maybe Poppy would comment, with her Wonder Woman levels of confidence, but Jess knew she didn't own that confidence anymore, if she ever had. Maybe it was all the mistakes she was making, but these days she seemed to live in second guessing land. Which was not ideal in filling a client with confidence that their vet knew what she was about. But Dr. Theo only tolerated so many interruptions to his day, so she didn't want to keep asking him. She found herself praying that God would make the answers plain, when sometimes her brain glitched over what to do.

Worry gnawed her sleep. At least with Franklin and Hannah out of the country she had their apartment to herself. But even though she enjoyed the luxury of a proper bed, and not the camp bed of the clinic or her car, still sleep refused to come.

Exhaustion lined her pores, brain fog regularly appeared, clearing only when she prayed. But even God felt far away.

Her phone rang as Paige entered, kitten in hand. Jess had a quick glance at the onscreen caller ID. Lisette. Again. She still hadn't answered the last time. Well, she'd tried to, but Lisette hadn't answered so she'd left a message. As Lisette would have to do because she had her hands full of kittens and couldn't respond right now. But there was no notification of a message, so maybe it wasn't important after all.

"Okay, let's deal with this one." She got Paige to hold the kitten as she administered the knock-out drugs and began the process of castration. The male kitten remained blissfully asleep, unaware that his life had changed forever. At least this one wouldn't sire litters. Millions of cats were destroyed across North America each year thanks to rampant population increases. Unwanted cats increased in number, while wanted veterinarians seemed unable to keep pace with demand. "It's a funny old world," she muttered, before suturing the last stitch. "There, that should do."

Her phone rang again. This time, Mom's name flashed across the screen. She frowned. Mom never rang during work hours. "Do you mind if I get it?" she asked Paige.

"I can finish up here," the veteran nurse said.

"Thanks." She stripped off her gloves and pressed answer. "Mom? What's wrong?"

Her mom's breath was shaky. "It's Buster."

"Buster?" Her heart clenched. "What's happened?"

"Oh, honey, I'm so sorry to tell you this, but he's gone."

"Gone? Gone where?" In the echo of her words her heart stabbed again. She grasped the side of the bench. "You mean he's died?"

"Yes, honey. I'm so sorry."

She blinked hard and pressed her lips together, turning away from the curious look Paige was giving her. "Um, how?"

"I don't know, honey. I'm so sorry. I realized after lunch I hadn't seen him all day, so I went to the barn and found he'd crawled behind a hay bale. He was cold when I found him, so he may have been there all night."

Her eyes filled, and she exhaled, rapidly blinking. Poor Buster. What a way to go, all alone, so cold. How awful. "He... he was old."

"It's never easy to lose a pet."

Oh, she knew that too well.

Emotion clawed at her, and she batted it away. She had to be strong. Be professional. She could just imagine what Dr. Theo would say if he saw her breaking down. *You're weak. We should find a replacement.*

Maybe he should—if he could find one.

"Jess, I'm so sorry," her mom said. "I hope you can come home this weekend. Cassie has said we'll wait for you before we bury him."

She sucked in another breath. Oh, she *was* weak. "I'll be there tomorrow." And if Dr. Theo insisted on otherwise she'd pull a sick day. That seemed to be the only way she got time off around here. That was probably what she should've done on Father's Day, rather than feel guilted into showing up then try to leave for the ranch only to get that phone call and return to work for a no-show. Who called an emergency number and begged to come in and then didn't? Her heart fisted in fresh frustration. Who did that?

"Jess, are you okay?" Paige asked.

"It's my mom," she whispered, covering the phone.

Paige's eyes were wide. "I'm so sorry. Was it your grandfather?"

"What?"

"Who died." Paige winced. "Sorry, I couldn't help but overhear."

"Oh no. It was my dog. But I'd had him since I was eighteen."

"He must've been very old."

How old did Paige think she was? Sure this job had aged her —she might've found a gray hair this morning to go with new lines around her eyes—but most dogs lived to thirteen or fourteen. Did Paige think she was over thirty?

"Sorry Mom, I need to go. But I'll get there tomorrow. Tonight, if I get out of here on time for once." She caught Paige's wince like she knew that wouldn't happen.

"I hope so, honey. I know this is hard. I wish Franklin was there to give you a hug. I know Buster was special to you."

"I think he's happy to be in Italy." And strangely, it wasn't Franklin's hug she craved, or even her mom or her father's. It was another man, someone who made her smile, who told dumb jokes that made her laugh. The man she'd sent away.

See? Dumb Jess. Not smart Jess. Dumb Jess who made dumb decisions.

She exhaled, rubbed her eyes, rubbed the moisture away. Faked a smile. "Okay, Paige, so what do we have next?"

As HE WAITED FOR A BITE, one bite, any bite, Tom scrolled through his phone, watching others living their best lives. Franklin in Italy with Hannah. The Spanish steps, the Trevi fountain, eating gelato, on a gondola in Venice. Yep, bucket list items all.

"It's a good thing he's having fun, huh?" He scratched Benji's head. "And a good thing we're not jealous."

"Who are you not jealous of?" his dad asked, adjusting his line as the boat bobbed on the lake.

"Franklin is in Italy with his wife."

"Living the dream, huh?"

"Yep."

"While you're stuck here with your old man."

"Hey, I didn't say that. I love you Dad, you know that."

"I do, and I love you too. Which is why I know you've been a little lonely."

Man, he hadn't done a good job hiding that then. "I've been having fun."

"I know. And it's been great having someone to swap bad jokes with."

Tom smiled. That had been fun.

"But I can understand you might want more than this. What's happening with your lady friend?"

"Franklin's sister?"

His dad's brows shot up. "Is there another?"

"No."

"Well, have you heard from her?"

Did a *Like* on an Instagram post count? If it was from her, that is. He didn't usually look at his comments, but he'd seen one from a jessjames and he'd instantly gone to look her up. No posts, as it was a private account, with no identifying picture except a messy-haired cute terrier. That account might be hers, but was it? He didn't want to message some random woman, especially if she was a fan. Things could get ugly really quick, or so their social media training had taught them. "Not really."

"What's she doing?"

"Working." Probably. Definitely. She didn't do anything else. *Lord, help her.* "That's what she does, it's who she is."

"Everyone needs a break once in a while. Otherwise they break."

His dad knew that only too well, having taken early retirement when his job at a RCAF base in Moose Jaw had proved too much. Smart investments over the years had seen his parents make the most of their retirement, before settling down so they could be ready for the grandbabies, when Michelle got busy.

And yeah, maybe Tom had gotten a little interested in the world of vets, thanks to a certain one in particular, but he'd noticed an article online lately that talked about the pressures faced by veterinarians. That they had one of the highest rates of suicide among professionals, thanks to a toxic mix of overwork and long hours, perfectionism that led to feelings of failure when they couldn't save an animal, and dealing with clients who couldn't pay or blamed the vet for disappointing outcomes. Vets often acted as shock absorbers, which took a toll. His heart panged, just as it had when he'd first read the article. *Lord, help Jess find strength in You.*

"You could go back," his dad said. "It's a statutory holiday soon."

"She'll probably still be working."

"Maybe, maybe not. You won't know unless you try."

"Yeah, she pretty much made it clear she doesn't want much to do with me."

"So? Are you a Chavez or not? You know what Chavez means? It means—"

"Keys, Dad, yeah I know"

"So you simply gotta find the key to her heart. Aww, listen to me, I sound like Michelle or your mother. I must be going soft."

"Must be."

"Hey." His dad gently punched him affectionately. "You're the soft one here. Just because a woman says no, it doesn't mean she means it."

"Yeah, Dad, that might've worked for you but I think you'll find the world is a different place from last century."

"I don't mean forcing her to do something she doesn't want, but forcing her to notice you isn't such a bad thing, is it?"

"We're friends."

"And that's a good starting point. The best starting point, actually. You can build a real good marriage on friendship."

Tom choked. "We're hardly at marriage yet, Dad. Don't get too excited. It'd just be nice if she agreed to go out on a date with me."

"Well how's she going to do that if you're here and she's there? Come on, Son. Use your brain. She needs to see you, right?"

"I said I'd stay here until Canada Day."

"Then go back and see her. And in the meantime let her know that you're still thinking of her. Not in a creepy way, but so she knows you care. You don't know what's going on in her life. She might really be needing a friend right now."

Maybe she was.

He flicked open his phone again. Found his Instagram post. Found her name. Should he? *Lord?*

He didn't sense a no, so he tapped on her name and wrote a message, like some creepy dude sliding randomly into a woman's DMs.

He hoped this was innocent enough, especially if he'd got the wrong girl.

Hope you're doing okay.

He waited a bit. Ah, what had he expected? As if she was sitting by her phone ready to instantly reply.

He snapped a pic of the lake and uploaded that, with the caption *Love summer in Canada.* Wondered if she'd reply. Or if she'd like it.

His line tugged, and he nearly dropped his phone. He placed it on the deck safely, then began reeling it in, standing, then bracing himself against the side, then reeling in his line.

"Hey, you got yerself a good walleye there," his dad crowed. "It's a beauty."

Tom grinned, and let his dad take his photo holding the fish, bare chest and all. Call him shallow, but he wasn't above using some tanned skin to see if he could draw somebody out. He put the fish in a bucket of water, ready to cook for dinner, then after cleaning up, uploaded the picture of him holding the fish, too, and checked his messages.

His heart pricked when he saw he had two. Then dropped as neither name was that of a famous gunslinger.

Franklin: *Hey, lake life looks good.*

Mike: *Livin' the dream.*

He exhaled. See, that was the problem with envy. Everyone somewhere in the world compared themselves to others instead of finding satisfaction with what they had. He bet there'd be a lot less violence in the world if people learned to find contentment in what they had.

Which was maybe what he should do, despite what his dad had said. Jess had made her intentions pretty clear, and he wanted to respect them, respect her.

Another message flashed. Luc Blanchard, from the Bible study chat: *Put those guns away, sir.*

He snickered. Okay, he might've flexed a little in the fish pic.

He tapped back to his pics. Saw two more likes from one more name. The very name he'd been hoping for. Then saw that same name had started typing a message in response to his. Then stopped.

Man, he hoped she was the right Jess. He had to encourage her. What could he say?

If it was her, then he knew what she'd respond to—one of the keys to her heart. He typed:

Cute dog.

He waited. Waited some more. Then had to help his dad as he reeled in his own fish. Then took another couple of pics, including a selfie with his dad looking proud as punch and with Benji in the foreground, and he uploaded those two, too.

Then checked his messages. And—his heart thumped—saw he had a reply.

Six

His name was Buster.

Jess eyed the message, chewing her lip. She should be working, but had felt the weirdest sense to check her phone—okay, to go look at Tom's Instagram account and see if he'd posted any more clues as to where he was. And then, boom, there he was. Dropping pictures of good times that so far hadn't included a single one with any blondes.

But had included a couple of a muscular chest she could tell matched equally distracting and muscular legs. He was having fun in the sun like a normal person, while she was here working like a slave. At least she'd had the weekend off to say her goodbye to Buster. The very pet whose face was memorialized in the profile pic she'd chosen for her Instagram account.

Was?

He'd replied again. Tears pricked. She glanced up but Dr. Theo and the others were nowhere around. She took another bite of her sandwich, eating very slowly. Paige had been kind to her lately, not rushing her to the next job as she'd done in the past. She wasn't due for her next appointment for another five minutes, which meant she had some time to reply.

> Buster died last Friday. 😿

> I'm really sorry. 😔🙏

Hot tears pricked again. She sensed the genuineness in his reply, with his sad face and praying hands emojis. Tom had said before he prayed for her. It was just as well he had been, because obviously she needed all the prayers she could get. If she hadn't had people praying for her, who knew what kind of basket case she'd be by now?

> Thanks.

All she could say.

> How are you doing?

He'd asked that before. She should probably answer.

> Life isn't as much fun as wherever it is you are.

> I'm in Saskatchewan with my family. It's pretty nice, except for listening to a baby crying through the night.

> Not ready to be a dad yet, huh?

She winced as her fingers accidentally tapped send and sent that through the atmosphere. Ugh. She sounded so forward, like she was begging him to consider her as a future mother to his kids.

> Can't wait, actually.

She blinked. Did he mean—?

> I mean, I can wait. Obviously. I meant I'm
> looking forward to that. One day.

Okay. Phew. Tom was a nice guy, and she didn't like to think of him having litters of children—wait, what was she doing, thinking like that?

"Jessie, your next client is here."

"Thanks, Paige." She stuffed the rest of the sandwich in her mouth and then faced a painful swallow. She'd bitten off too much. In her sandwich, in her work, and maybe in this conversation.

But oh, it was good to talk to Tom, even if it was only by message. It'd be even better to see him in person. Which reminded her.

> Hey, you know you're welcome to come back
> to dog training school. I was joking about you
> not coming before.

😁 I'd planned to.

Her heart thumped.

> Good. People have missed you.

Her finger hovered over the send key. Would he think she meant herself? While it was true, she didn't want him misinterpreting things.

> Margaret especially.

she added, making it clear.

He took a little longer to reply this time, and she knew she had to get back to work. But didn't want to keep wondering about what he might reply.

> I've gotta get back to the grindstone. Thank you for talking.

His messages came back straightaway. Obviously he'd been composing it while she'd been typing.

> How about you?

Her heart caught. Was he asking if she had missed him?

> Any time.

Was that in response to her most recent message?

"Jessie!"

At Dr. Theo's yell she fumbled her phone and it fell onto the floor with a crack. She winced and picked it up. Sure enough, a lovely jagged crack now splintered the screen. She shoved it away. Saw another call from Lisette. The woman was persistent. She'd call her back as soon as her shift ended.

"Get in here now!" Dr. Theo bellowed.

"I'm coming!"

Welcome to another day in paradise.

IT WAS—UNSURPRISINGLY—LATE by the time Dr. Theo finally let her go. She stumbled to her car, glad for its cocoon-like ability to shield her from the world. Tonight would consist of a drive-thru dinner, then back to Franklin's to sleep, but first she'd check her phone to see if a certain somebody had left a message. He'd only sent a smiley face, which seemed most appropriate for him. He was that kind of guy, fun, funny, generous, a Christian, good-hearted, family oriented. Everything her teenage self had dreamed of in a one-day husband. Not that she could contemplate that. But maybe, if she could keep this friendship ticking along for another few years, she might finally emerge from this train wreck of a job and actually be one of those ones who could leave work at six instead of past seven. Apparently all she'd need to leave on time was to be a parent of young children, so having a husband might be helpful for that.

"You're so pathetic," she muttered. "How would Tom feel if he knew you wanted a husband simply so you could make your work-life balance easier?"

See? Proof that her job was killing her, because it was obviously killing any brain cells that worked. She wasn't even making sense now. If she couldn't even juggle her work responsibilities without kids, how on earth would she manage with kids and husband to juggle as well? She was obviously going insane.

It must be time to eat.

She got something suitably non-nutritious via drive-thru and ate it in the car, parking in Franklin's apartment's car spot, then taking the elevator to his floor. Then remembered she was supposed to call Lisette back. "Hopefully she's free now too."

She pressed return call, but there was no answer. Tried again, in case she was busy. This time she left a message. "Hey, Lisette, I hate playing phone tag with you, but I tried to call. Hope you're doing well. We should definitely catch up sometime soon. Okay, bye."

Just to be on the safe side she sent a message as well, saying much the same. Then had a shower and went to sleep.

THE NEXT DAY she finally had a moment to grab a coffee and check her phone. Sure enough, Tom had sent a sunrise shot over water, which meant she sent a photo of her desk.

He then sent one of Benji, and she sent one of the dog school pamphlet.

Her phone rang, and recognizing the number as Lisette's she

hastily answered. "Lisette! I'm so glad to finally talk to you. What's it been, weeks now of missing each other? Months? How are you?"

There was silence for a long moment.

Weird. "Lisette? Are you there?"

A sniffling sound came on the other end of the phone.

"Lisette? Whatever's the matter I'm sure we can sort it out."

"It's too late," a voice said that she didn't recognize.

Fear clutched her heart. "Who is this?"

"This is Lisette's mother. Lisette has..." A shuddery breath. "Gone."

"Gone where?" she asked slowly.

"Lisette..." Another shaky breath. "Oh, I can't believe I'm saying this. Lisette... killed herself last night."

The world tilted. What? Killed herself? This had to be a joke. But... who would joke about something like that? And the sniffling—was that faked? "Lisette's mother?" She had vague memories of a beautiful woman who at graduation had stood so proudly next to her daughter as she'd shaken hands with the dean of students.

"I didn't know." The woman was openly crying now. "I didn't know how hard she was finding things."

"No. She can't be dead."

Paige passed her and offered a sympathetic smile. Like she had when she'd heard about Buster. But there was a world of difference between mourning the loss of an old dog and the shock of discovering a friend had killed herself. Tears sprang, a sick churning began in her stomach.

This couldn't be true. It couldn't. It *couldn't!*

How many times had Lisette tried to contact her? How many times had she put her off and not gotten back to her? Been too busy. Made excuses. Oh, she was such a bad friend, bad friend, a bad friend.

She took a shaky breath. "I'm so sorry."

"I didn't know she felt this way," Lisette's mom wailed.

She closed her eyes at the raw pain she could hear. "I didn't know either."

"If only I'd listened."

Regrets poured over her, pecking at her, like the birds that pecked at the eyeballs of roadkill.

"Jessie—are you on your phone again?" Dr. Theo glared.

"Someone has died," Paige stage-whispered.

"Is this another of your pets? A goldfish perhaps." He rolled his eyes.

How unfeelingly cruel was this man? She covered the phone, smothering the sound of Lisette's mom's tears. "A friend from university. She was in my class at school. Her mother is on the line."

How strange to say 'was' when Lisette had always been so full of life. *Had* been. Past tense. And now she wasn't here. And Jess didn't even know if Lisette had ever prayed the prayer that secured eternal life. Right now she couldn't remember if she'd ever told Lisette about how to find hope in Jesus. So was she in heaven now —or hell?

Nausea rose up, and she snatched a nearby trash can and vomited.

"That's disgusting. You'll need to clean that up."

"Dr. Theodore," Paige began, "Jessie has had a shock, and I really think perhaps she should go home, and—"

"She can go home."

She could? Oh, she'd never thought she'd say it but God bless the man.

"After she's cleaned up this mess, and after she's finished her shift. We're short-staffed today enough as it is."

"But—"

"No, Paige, I've had enough of this young woman's attitude."

"Dr. Theo—"

"Please do not interrupt me." His eyes flashed. "I do not like it when a subordinate feels like they dare interrupt me."

Jess slumped in her seat, head bowed, as the whip of his words continued to flay. She was irresponsible. She was a bad friend. She had failed. Failed to be a real friend. Failed as a Christian to share the good news. Instead she'd indulged in envy and comparison and pride and wanting just a tenth of what Lisette had seemed to have. Had *seemed* to have, because obviously those things she'd had hadn't been enough to keep her satisfied. Oh, poor Lisette. Poor Lisette's mom.

She glanced at her phone, and sure enough, earned a roar of disapproval from Dr. Theo. Lisette's mom must've ended the call. She hoped she'd gone before Dr. Theo had started berating Jess. The poor woman didn't need more angst in her life.

Lord, be with her. Be with Lisette's family. I'm so sorry I wasn't a better friend. Tears leaked, and she wiped them away.

Eventually the noise of Dr. Theo's voice left, and she felt a cool hand on her shoulder. She glanced up. Paige. Her own eyes shiny with tears. "I'm so sorry Jess. Was she a good friend?"

"Not really," she whispered. "And that makes me feel worse. I should've been a better friend to her."

"I'm so sorry Dr. Theo is being like this. He's quite stressed at the moment."

Weren't they all?

"And I'm sure he didn't mean half of what he said."

Yeah, nothing sure about that. She'd heard him say similar things too many times before.

"Go wash yourself up, and I'll do my best to give the rest of your afternoons to others. You need to have the weekend off. And don't worry, let me know when the funeral is and I'll be sure to get you the day off for that too."

"Thanks."

She felt wobbly, but made her way to the bathroom. Washed her face. Rinsed her mouth. Braced against the cold porcelain sink as a hundred questions flew through her brain, all without answers.

Lord, I've got nothing. I need You to help me. Please, help me get through this day.

And she pushed herself up from the sink and slowly made her way back to the office.

TOM MIGHT'VE HAD a fun time these last few days, enjoying time with his family, learning the joys of diaper changing like a good uncle, and watching Canada Day fireworks over Lake Waskesiu, but anticipation rode high as he and Benji made the trek back to Calgary.

He couldn't wait to see Jess again. It felt like years, even though it had only been weeks. But the past few messages felt like their friendship had taken some more steps towards deepening into something more real. Even if she had been silent since last Friday.

He'd figured work was busy for her, and because he didn't want to stress her out by pushing too much, he thought showing up at dog training and surprising her might be a better bet.

He rubbed Benji's head. "I think she'll enjoy seeing you again, even if she's not so sure about me."

Benji barked an Amen.

"You might need to give her some love, seeing as she sounds like she's missing her dog." What was its name again? "Buster."

Benji woofed.

Tom grinned. Benji's mild manner had seen Michelle hint that Tom should return Benji to their home, but he'd steered her off each time conversation headed that way. Her apartment was too small, he reminded her, which was why he had Benji now. Besides, Benji didn't need to be treated like a yo-yo. The dog was confused enough, thinking Michelle and Travis were taking him back. Although, now he thought about it, what would he do with Benji once the season started and he had long road trips that kept him out of town for days at a time? Maybe that was another topic of conversation he could have with Jess, something that would bond them a little closer. She might know a good place he could board Benji, or she might even be willing to take him herself. Not that he wanted to overstep or intrude but it could be a good way to stay connected, especially with him surprising her at dog training tomorrow night.

"Hey God, can You have Your way with all this?" he prayed.

He pressed the accelerator. He couldn't wait to see her.

"YOU'RE BACK!" Margaret said as he pulled up beside her in the vet clinic's parking lot the next night. "We thought you'd left."

"I had some family things to do. Hey, Jarrett!" Tom waved to the kid and his mom.

"Hi Tom."

Jarrett's beaming smile that could light a night sky said Jess had been right. He had been missed. Aww…

"What have you been learning about lately?"

Jarrett and Margaret told him about their latest dog school lessons, and Jarrett demonstrated just how well his dog could now sit.

"Good for you, bud. He's really doing well now."

"Right?"

He noticed a few people standing at the vet clinic's front door, and moved to join them. Then read the sign attached to the glass.

Dog training lessons cancelled tonight due to a funeral.

She wasn't here? He wouldn't see her? Disappointment swooped, chased by new concern. Was she okay? Poor thing. He hoped it wasn't anyone too close to her.

"A funeral?" Margaret shook her head. "You'd think Dr. James would have given us more notice."

"Or sent out a text message," one of the blondes said.

"Perhaps she didn't have much advance warning," he suggested.

The blonde peeked up at him, flicked her hair. "Hi Tom. Good to see you again."

He dipped his chin, as the murmurs continued.

"Whose funeral do you think it was?"

"Why didn't she let us know before now?"

"It's not very professional if you ask me."

His heart ached for her. Her dog's recent loss, then this; she was going through a hard time. No wonder she hadn't responded to his latest message. She must be feeling a little battered by life right now. He wished he had the right to hug her, that he could impart some of his strength to her. *Lord, be with her, comfort her, bring her peace.*

Some of the women were muttering about something they'd seen on Facebook, and while he didn't like gossip he couldn't help but overhear some words. "Vet graduate." "Overdose." "Same class."

And while he'd had a few pucks to the head over the years, it didn't take a genius to put two and two together. Had a friend of hers overdosed? *Oh, poor Jess.*

He turned from the temptation to ask the women for their sources, and scratched Benji's head instead. "Well, it looks like we don't have classes now, so we might as well get you home."

Benji barked, and he caught how some of the others smiled.

"He's such a good dog," Margaret said.

"Woof woof."

"Look, he heard you," Jarrett said. He glanced at Tom. "Can I pat him?"

"Thanks for asking. Yes, you can."

Jarrett held out a hand for Benji to sniff, and Benji licked him, which drew Jarrett's shriek of laughter, and caused a momentary lift in Tom's heart.

But as he drove away, he soon fell back to wondering how Jess was doing, and how he could be a blessing for her in this challenging time. And whether he should manufacture an excuse to call in and see her tomorrow. Just as a friend, of course.

He rolled his eyes at himself. But if friendship was what she wanted, then that was what he'd give. That, and continued prayers for God to sustain her and help her and bring comfort. "In Jesus's name."

Seven

Grief like a dense fog clouded her heart and mind. Guilt, a heavy weight, oppressed her. One might think that months of reduced sleep might prepare her for the past week, but it hadn't. She'd barely slept since Monique, Lisette's mom, had called last Friday. And while she'd thought that conversation was tremendously hard, nothing had prepared her for the awfulness of Lisette's funeral.

Oh, she *never* wanted to attend another funeral of a non-Christian again. Where was the hope? Where was the assurance of heaven? Monique and her husband had talked about Lisette's beauty, her accomplishments, her outstanding achievement, but it all seemed like wisps of vapor, here one minute, gone the next. What was the point in working so hard if she'd just ended her life? What was the point in anything, if her eternity was not secured?

Guilt gnawed, reminding Jess she should've said something, should have talked about Jesus, shared about her faith. But she hadn't. Not much, anyway. And now, unless by some miracle Lisette had made a commitment years ago, it seemed the valedictorian of her class was spending an eternity in hell, while Jess lived here in a different version of it. Chased by regrets. Shame. Sorrow.

She'd cried so much after the funeral she'd had to call Paige and ask her to cancel the dog class. She didn't have it in her. "I thought I could, but I just can't. And now I feel bad to not call people and give them warning."

"It's okay, we'll put a sign up. You're doing the right thing," Paige had said. "You need to be kind to yourself."

She should've been kinder to Lisette. Should have answered her calls. Should have made the effort to respond to someone who had clearly wanted to connect. Oh, if only she had, Lisette might still be alive...

Lord, I'm sorry, I'm sorry, I'm so sorry.

But it felt like her prayers hit the ceiling and ricocheted back down. God felt so far away.

DR. THEO's compassion extended to granting leave—at Paige's insistence—for Jess to have an afternoon off for the funeral. "But I expect you back on Friday morning, just as usual."

She'd nodded, then had to drag herself from bed, shivering, even though it was a warm day. Maybe she was coming down with something. If she was sick then maybe she could avoid work for a few more days.

But no. She wasn't sick. Except maybe sick at heart.

She hadn't told her parents much beyond the fact that Lisette had died. Mom had been instantly sympathetic. Dad had understood, and told her to take care of herself.

But she couldn't get the image out of her head of poor Monique sobbing over her daughter's coffin. Or the way she'd found Jess after, and begged her to be careful.

"I heard how that man spoke to you on the phone. Don't let yourself be bullied by men like that. I think that was part of what troubled Lisette so." She'd grasped Jess's hands, her eyes wide, wild. "I know you think your job is important, but no job is important enough if you think it becomes more important than life."

She'd nodded, felt the sting of conviction. Her dad had said something similar. Her mom, too. Yet old habits were hard to break, conscientiousness and duty like twin railway tracks her life slid along.

So quitting was a nice idea, but it wasn't as simple as that. Quitting felt like failure. Besides, she'd signed a contract. She had responsibilities. People relied on her. She couldn't give up. Couldn't fail.

Her head felt full of cotton wool, her limbs ached, but she forced one step in front of the other. Forced herself to nod, pay attention to the clients who had booked appointments, forced herself to think through weight that felt like chains inside.

"Jess, are you sure you should be here?" Paige asked.

"What choice do I have?"

If she stayed at home, she'd just dissolve in tears. At least here she had the distraction of doing, doing, doing that forced her to put aside her regrets for a few minutes at a time.

So she struggled through her morning, kept her tears for the bathroom during lunch, and started her afternoon, thankful that Dr. Theo had been called away. Even if it meant she'd be stuck here doing an extra hour or so. At least she wouldn't be at home, crying. Her lips twisted. "You can cry here instead."

Another hour passed. Dog exams. Cat injections. She felt weighted, heavy, yet fragile.

Another hour. Grief pressed in. She blinked it back. Had to wipe at a stray tear.

Several of the other staff left, making the most of their Friday half days. Not her, though. She had the delights of putting down Daisy, a poor dog who likely would have lived if their owner had been able to afford the treatment. Why did people have pets they couldn't afford to keep?

"Paige?" one of the other nurses called. "There's an urgent phone call for you." Paige hurried away, then quickly returned to the exam room, clutching her phone.

"Jessie, that was my daughter. She was just involved in a car crash. I need to go pick her up."

Car crash? The words sounded like they came from far away. *Come on, girl. Think.* What was she supposed to say? That's right. "Is she okay?"

"She's shaken up. Her car was hit by a probationary driver."

Poor thing. Poor both drivers, actually. Her heart—weary as it was—stirred in compassion for the new driver who no doubt would be feeling the challenge of never wanting to drive again. "It's okay. I'll lock up."

"Are you sure? Mrs. Mildrew is out the front with Patty. She's the last, unless there are any walk-ins."

"Go. Your daughter needs you." And having seen Monique's grief, she never wanted to be the person who came between a mother and her child again. "I'll be praying for her."

"Thanks so much."

Jess's prayers followed Paige as she exited out the back door. Which left her here, alone, except for the poor dumped creature, and Mrs. Mildrew waiting out front, with the angry pampered cat with a heart condition because it was overfed.

Honestly, some people didn't deserve to own pets. She rubbed a hand over poor Daisy's head, unable to look her in the eyes. "I'm so sorry your life has been like this," she murmured. There was nothing to be done. If her owners had sought help weeks ago, they might have got a treatment plan to work, but they hadn't, and now it was too late.

Her eyes filled, her hands shaking as she retrieved the syringe and administered the lethal dose. One blink, two blinks, then Daisy shuddered and moaned and grew very still.

Tears slipped from her eyelids. But she had to be professional. She couldn't break down, even though she felt so fragile. She still had Mrs. Mildrew and Patty to see. A pet owner who was killing her cat with what she thought was kindness, while this poor animal had just been put down due to a lack of kindness. Oh, this world was so wrong.

The dark swirl of anxiety pressed in. A roll call of the animals she'd needed to put down flashed before her. What an awful job this was. So much death. So much pain. So much suffering. She might save the occasional animal but it was simply too little. She might as well be plugging the river wall with her thumb while ahead of her the broken banks spilled millions of megaliters. Ready to drown her.

She blinked hard, her eyes lifting to poor Daisy, then did what needed to be done. After carrying her to the deep freezer where the body would remain until the cremation company came, she cleaned up, stripped off her gloves, then braced against the counter. Deep breath in. She could do this. Slow exhale. And release. Let it go. Move onto the next one.

But how many more animals would she personally be responsible for ending their lives? This wasn't why she had signed up to become a vet. "I want to save lives, not end them," she whispered.

Pain and sorrow, her twin companions these many days, reared up, reminding her of her failures. Her faults. Her shortcomings. So many, many of them. When pet owners had yelled at her, blamed her. When Dr. Theodore had done the same, basically confirming what she suspected herself. That she was incompetent. Useless. Untalented.

Regrets roared. She might once have thought herself smart, but she knew now how much she didn't know. She couldn't do this job. She could barely stay afloat in life. Was this how poor Lisette had felt, feeling the constant pressure to perform then realizing how much she couldn't meet expectations?

She eyed the cabinet where the drugs were kept then instantly averted her face. No. It wasn't that bad. *Not yet*, an inner voice whispered.

"Stop." Her fingers clutched the edge. "You need to get a grip. Mrs. Mildrew is waiting. This is normal, to be expected."

But, but... it didn't feel normal to her.

Not with another poor creature gone. Oh, this was so unfair. Her skin goose-pimpled, as her internal shivers shuddered to her skin. She was shivering. She couldn't do this anymore. This was so wrong. So much. Too much. Too hard. "God?"

Her fingers let go, and she slid down against the cupboard and huddled on the floor, silently wailing on the floor.

TOM PUSHED OPEN the vet clinic's waiting room doors, Benji leashed by his side. "There you go, boy."

Benji trotted in obediently, and Tom nodded to the lone occupant, a middle aged woman holding a sour expression not dissimilar to that worn by her disgruntled fat cat. Maybe it was true that owners ended up looking like their pets.

He rubbed a hand over Benji's ears. "Good thing you're such a handsome boy, then, huh?"

Benji barked, as if in agreement. Tom's smile faded as the woman sighed loudly.

"Dr. James is running late. Again." She shook her head. "I don't know why I keep coming here. They're late every time."

"They're popular because they're the best."

The woman muttered something Tom didn't catch, but it sounded like Jess could do with more defending. He rubbed Benji's ears, pulling at them gently in the way that almost made Benji purr like a cat, then said loud enough so the woman could hear, "We're both big fans of Dr. James, aren't we?"

The seconds ticked by, and the woman's cat hissed, clawing awareness that the absent receptionist was taking an awfully long time. It was technically now after hours, but even so, he was used to seeing someone on desk duty to lock up.

"What time was your appointment?" he asked the woman.

"It was supposed to be twenty minutes ago. But I haven't seen anyone for the last fifteen minutes." She huffed. "The receptionist got a phone call then left and I haven't seen her since."

"It must've been an emergency."

"Why they have to choose my appointment time to have an emergency is beyond me." She folded her arms.

He figured that pointing out the unreasonableness of that

comment was unlikely to be appreciated, so scrolled through his phone. Saw the Northwest Ice chat had exploded in a bunch of funny memes—a meme-off, as Ryan Guillemette called it.

Luc's joke: *Why are Canadians so good at hockey? They always bring their "eh" game*, drew a smile.

As did Mike's joke: *How many police officers does it take to change a light bulb? None. They wait for it to turn itself in.*

Memes and jokes distracted him for a while, but Benji was getting a little antsy. Where was the receptionist? Where was Jess? After missing seeing her, thanks to the cancelled class last night, he'd hoped this would be a nice surprise after a stressful week. Now it looked like the surprise was on him.

Concern pricked at him as another five minutes passed with no word. He glanced at the sour-faced woman. "I might go check out back."

"Better you than me. The last time I dared say anything that young Dr. James gave me what for."

He pressed his lips together, so he didn't say anything he might regret.

Like, he knew only too well Jessie James's proclivity for straight shooting.

Or the fact that Dr. James had the veterinary degree, not this woman.

Or if Dr. James was telling this woman things she didn't want to hear, then it was likely for a good reason.

Or that this woman didn't seem the type to like to hear anything but what she wanted.

"I'll be back in a moment." That was safe.

He knocked on the staff door, then pushed it open. "Dr. James?"

The hall was silent. He went through, and closed the door, motioning for the curious woman to stay, even as Benji huddled close to his side.

"Come on boy, let's find her."

He peered through the half-frosted glass panel insert on an

exam room door. Nothing.

Man, he hoped she wouldn't be upset by him tiptoeing around here. And he really hoped her awful boss wasn't lurking about. Agitation grew. Was that the problem? Had her boss hit on her? Had a client got upset and yelled at her? She'd shared some stories before, and it seemed some pet owners were even more passionate than hockey fans about how things should be done.

A muffled noise drew him to the next room. He knocked and peered through the glass insert. Benji started pawing the door, so Tom opened it.

Benji raced inside, barking, going behind the counter. Tom followed.

"Jess!"

She was crumpled on the floor, shuddering, her cheeks stained with tears. Had someone attacked her? Had her boss—?

He rushed to kneel beside her. "Jess, what's happened? What's wrong? Do I need to call 911?"

She didn't say anything, only curled deeper within herself.

His heart wrenched. He'd never seen her lose control like this. She was always so calm, so contained. *Dear Lord, help her. What do I do?* He gingerly touched her hair. "Has someone hurt you?"

She shook her head, eyes still shut.

Relief whooshed through him. *Thank You, God.* "What can I do?" he murmured, daring to smooth a strand of hair behind her ear.

She didn't answer, only held out a hand. He grasped it, and she clutched it like she might a lifeline. That was enough for him to move beside her and murmur, "Hey, come here."

She let him sweep her up, and he repositioned himself with her in his arms, his back in the corner as he sat on the cold tiled floor. She huddled close to his chest, and he soothed her, rubbing her back gently, and pressed his lips to the crown of her head. "It's okay, Jess. You're safe. I'm here. I won't let anything hurt you."

Her hand curled, clutching his t-shirt, as her wet face pressed against his chest. Could she feel how fast his heart was beating?

He'd never expected to get quite this up close and personal when he'd arrived here today.

What had happened? Had yesterday's funeral proved too much? Or—his stomach swooped—was this the result of her job being too much? The article he'd read about burnout among veterinarians sprang to mind. He drew her closer still, stroked her back and closed his eyes, praying for peace, for calm. She was so cold. Eventually the trembling slowed, then finally—*thank You, Lord*—ceased.

She dragged in a steadier breath. Another. Then groaned.

"What is it?" he murmured.

"I snotted on your shirt."

"You can snot on my shirt anytime you like."

She shuddered out a half-laugh, but that seemed to trigger new tears. "I'm such a mess."

"Actually, we're now both a mess."

His joke fell flat as her tears resumed in earnest. "I'm s-s-sorry."

"Hey, no. I was joking. I'm sorry. That was dumb." He pressed another kiss to her hairline. "What can I do to help?"

"This." She snuggled closer. "This is helping."

As much as it might be helping her, it was starting to get a little uncomfortable for him. Not because the floor was cold—he was used to sprawling on the ice—but because it had been a long time since he'd had a woman in his arms. And this woman, well... He didn't know what had happened to her, but she was his friend, and while part of him might want to make the most of this opportunity to hold her, he'd beat down the temptation for more.

He sure hoped nobody came in. It would look awfully compromising to anyone who might walk through the door.

He shifted, and she seemed to take that as his desire for her to get off his lap, as she inched away.

"I'm too heavy."

"Hey no, it's okay." She was so light. Almost too light. Like she hadn't been eating much lately. He wrapped his arms around her, savoring the fact she trusted him enough to let him care for her this way.

She nestled back in, her palm flat against his chest, and closed her eyes. From this angle he could see the teardrops lingering on her dark lashes. His heart thudded. Oh, he cared about this woman. Would do anything to help her. Be her body pillow for the rest of her days if that's what she wanted.

Benji, who had been looking on with concern, trotted nearer, and laid his head on her lap. Which was unfortunate timing as she lowered her hand from Tom's chest and stroked his dog's head instead.

They sat like that for a few blissful moments. Then Benji's ears pricked, and Tom heard a tap on the door.

"Hello?"

Shoot. The woman from the waiting room. He gently stroked Jess's face. "Hey Jess. Wake up."

Jess stirred, her blinks slow. "What's happening?"

Benji barked, which seemed to prove incentive for the woman to barge in.

"Jess," Tom whispered urgently. This wouldn't look good if the woman saw them seated on the floor, Jess on his lap.

"Oh, so you are in here, after all." The woman's voice grew louder. "I thought that door might be the Tardis and people disappeared, and—oh!" The woman peered down, her expression askance.

Tom's cheeks heated. "Dr. James is unwell." Yeah, even to his own ears it sounded weak.

"Well, she certainly is *something*."

Jess stiffened, her face creasing in a wince that said this latest arrival was unwelcome.

Which meant the woman had to go away. *Lord, please get this woman away.*

Just then, the cat hissed and crawled up her arms. "Patty, stop."

Tom cleared his throat. "I don't think Dr. James is any position to see Patty today."

The woman sniffed. "That is obvious."

At the way she eyed them, he was reminded of just how close they were sitting, and subtly eased Jess off, putting inches between them. "Dr. James needs to go home—"

"And that's with you, is it?"

"Jess is my friend, and I will be taking her to her family," he said firmly. *Lord, please don't let her blab about this to others.* "I'm sure the clinic will be able to reschedule you an appointment tomorrow."

"I'm glad *you* think they can. When I think of the trouble I had getting this one—"

"If you'll excuse us." He shifted, so his back was to her, and refocused his attention on Jess, blocking the inquisitive woman from her view.

She fixed her gaze on him, her eyes red-rimmed and tear-smudged. "I'm so sorry."

"Don't apologize. You have nothing to be sorry for."

"Yes, she does," the woman called.

"You do not," he said, willing Jess to believe him.

After a long moment, she finally nodded, then lowered her head.

He stayed like this for a moment, until he heard footsteps and the faint sound of the front door's chime that signaled the woman had likely left. *Thank You Jesus.* "Come on. Let's get you home."

She moved slowly, like his grandmother—God rest her soul—used to when she struggled to stand. So he scooped her up, again conscious of her weightlessness, and carried her outside, then took her to his Jeep.

"Benji will keep you company while I lock up. Where are your keys?"

She described their location, and that of her bag, and he jogged back inside, and called the emergency number on the receptionist desk. Weirdly, it rang through to Jessie's own phone, stashed in her bag he'd discovered in an office.

He switched off lights then used her keys to lock up, then returned to his car, and gave Jess her possessions. "I rang the emergency number which went to your phone. So you're the emergency contact?"

She'd slumped against the window, her eyes remaining closed. "It's my scheduled evening to do so."

"Your schedule sucks. Big time."

Her lower lip wobbled as she nodded.

Aww. Poor thing. She was obviously over-worked and stressed to the eyeballs. His fingers clenched. Her boss had a lot to answer for. "What's your boss's name?"

"Theodore."

He found it in her phone's contacts, then tapped the number. A man's tired voice snapped, "Jessica? What is it now?"

"This is Tom Chavez, Jessica's friend. I called in at the clinic and found that Jess is unwell so I'm taking her home." He didn't care about differentiating where that home might be. He had the feeling that the less this man knew about her whereabouts the less he'd hound her.

"But the clinic—"

"Is locked up, lights are off. You'll need to reschedule some woman and her angry cat tomorrow."

"But, but—"

Tom ended the call, then when the phone buzzed immediately with Theodore's name on-screen, he ended the call then put the phone on silent.

"Was that him?" Jess murmured, her eyes still closed.

"You don't need to worry about work right now," he assured. "Just relax, and we'll be at Three Creeks really soon."

He plugged in her seatbelt for her, then drove her carefully to her parents, praying all the way. Should he call them and give a heads up about what to expect? No. They were the kind of folks who'd want to see their daughter, and would help, no questions asked. Should he call Franklin, letting him know his sister wasn't well? Yeah, Franklin might not be too thrilled to know the two of them were close enough friends for Tom to do this. Besides, Jess might be embarrassed about too many people knowing. It was probably best he kept his mouth closed.

So he prayed instead. Prayed for her to know peace, to get rest, to find strength. And prayed for his own strength and wisdom to be the kind of friend she needed.

It took just under an hour to reach the tall poplars that marked the entrance to Three Creek Ranch. He drove under the wooden ranch gate sign, and saw the two-story homestead in the distance, near the red barn. The lights were low, indicating someone was home. He knew Derek and Leonie were early to bed folk, and hoped they would be understanding about why he'd done what he'd done. He wound down the windows and told Benji to stay, gently woke Jess, hopped out and moved to her door, then gently scooped her up in his arms.

A figure silhouetted the yellow light behind the opened front door. "Hello?"

At Derek's raspy call, Tom felt the nerves skitter through his veins. He sure hoped the man would understand why he was carrying his daughter in his arms like this. "Sir, it's Tom Chavez. I'm here with Jess."

"Jessie?" Leonie appeared now, wrapped in a cotton bathrobe. "Oh my! What's happened?"

"Jess fell ill at the clinic today." He hoisted her higher, and her face tipped against his chest.

"She's sick? Has she seen a doctor?"

"No." He eyed her. "I don't think she's physically ill, apart from a solid dose of exhaustion. I think what she really needs is rest."

Leonie bit her lip, met his gaze and nodded. "I knew she was working too hard." She touched Jess's face.

"Mom," Jess whispered, her eyelids fluttering open.

"Come on. Bring her upstairs. Then you can tell me everything."

Eight

Tom tiptoed down the farmhouse's steps, but they still creaked as he made his way back to the kitchen. He'd left Leonie to minister to Jess in her room—one glimpse at her bedroom was enough for him to know he shouldn't stay. Lingering meant more room for his imagination to go places where it shouldn't. Like imagining they were married and he had the right to tuck her in, to care for her. Talking with Derek should tamp down any speculation he should not indulge in.

Light and muted clatter took him to the kitchen, a squeaky floorboard saw Derek turn from where he was rinsing bowls at the sink. "How is she?"

"She's exhausted, out like a light already."

Derek leveled an assessing gaze at Tom which made him wonder what he saw.

He finally dipped his chin, and Tom relaxed a smidge. It seemed maybe he'd passed whatever test that was.

"Want a coffee?" Derek asked. "Something stronger? There's beer in the fridge."

"Thanks, but I haven't eaten and don't want to drink on an empty stomach."

His mouth curved to a quarter moon. "That a hint?"

"No. Not at all. I'll eat something when I get back home."

"You can eat something now if you want. Leonie made chili con carne. There's still some in the pot. We were cleaning up when you came by."

"I couldn't—"

"You can. Least we can do for the man who helped my Jessie," he said gruffly. "Now sit."

Tom obeyed as Derek moved to the stove and ladled out several portions in a bowl, microwaved it a minute, then pushed the bowl and a spoon and fork at him. "I'll rustle you up some toast too. Help yourself to the fixings." He gestured to the sour cream, hot sauce, and grated cheese.

Tom decorated half the bowl appropriately, then spooned in a mouthful. "This is really good."

"Right? Leonie knows how to make a meal stick to the sides of a man's belly."

Tom lifted his spoon, grateful for the chance to hide his bemusement behind another mouthful. Was this the most Derek had ever spoken to him? He'd gotten to know Jess's parents a little bit in the past year, but mostly at games or at Franklin's wedding, which had been pretty busy.

He concentrated on eating, while his thoughts strayed back upstairs. Was Jess still sleeping? Would she be okay? She *had* to be okay.

"Oh, good. You're eating something." Leonie touched Tom's shoulder.

He straightened. "How is she?"

"Still asleep." She waved for him to keep eating. "I know you're like Franklin, with a healthy appetite, regardless of whether you're playing."

"'fraid so."

"Whereas Jessica doesn't seem like she's been eating." Her brow pleated. "She's skin and bone."

"She's really light. I think her work hours have been crazy."

She nodded. "Work has been really hard for her. And then Buster died, then Lisette."

"Lisette?"

"She was in Jess's graduating class. She overdosed last week. They... the authorities don't believe it was accidental."

His heart wrenched afresh. The funeral yesterday. "Poor Jess."

He remembered that article he'd read about suicide rates in veterinarians being among the highest of all professions. That same compassion that drew people into this caring profession also led to burnout and fatigue as vets wrestled with dealing with more and more pet owners who often took out their frustrations and pain on vets who were simply trying to help them. No wonder Jess was exhausted. Her huge well of compassion must be close to dry.

"Can you tell us what happened tonight?"

"She didn't say anything?"

Leonie shook her head.

So he told them, sparing no details, not even the phone call with Dr. Theodore.

Leonie covered her mouth with her hands, then whispered "Oh no" as he described what had happened.

"Her phone is still in the car, and her bag." And Benji. "Actually, do you mind if I go get them? Benji, my dog, is there too, and I don't think Dr. Jess will be too pleased to know that I left him unattended all this time."

"She's already asleep, but you can bring him inside. It's not like we're unused to animals here."

"I'll be right back."

Benji was ecstatic to be released, and went around sniffing the yard until Tom called him to heel. They went inside and he handed over Jess's bag and phone, noting that there were a half dozen missed calls, five of them from Theodore. He gestured to it. "Her boss is pretty persistent. Apparently she was supposed to be on call tonight."

Leonie's eyes flashed. "That man should be ashamed of himself. Working her to the bone like that."

"I don't think she needs to be thinking about work right now."

"Exactly." She studied him. "Thank you for helping her. You're a good friend to her."

He swallowed, wishing he could say something about how he wished to be more. But that was a conversation he should have with Jess first. He didn't want her feeling like he'd manipulated her by having a conversation about their relationship with her parents first.

Derek motioned to Tom's half eaten bowl. "Better get the rest of that into you, Son."

Son. Derek's word reminded him he needed to call his own parents soon. Ask them to pray for Jess. And ask them not to tell Michelle. He didn't need her commentary adding to the whirl of emotions revolving like a carousel in his head.

"Would Benji like something to eat?" Leonie asked. "We have a bone here."

"If you feed Benji that, I'm afraid you won't ever get rid of him."

Leonie patted Benji's head, who looked up at her with beseeching eyes like he'd found a new best friend. "He's a sweet boy. Well behaved, too."

"He had an excellent teacher."

"You?" Derek asked.

"My sister," he admitted. "Then your daughter. That's actually how we got to know each other more this year. She was running dog obedience classes, as part of the clinic's after-hours courses, and she and Benji took a shine to each other."

"Benji, is it?" Derek asked. At Tom's nod, he continued. "A dog can have the best teacher in the world, but its behavior reflects its master's. So you must be doing something right."

His heart glowed at the validation from the man he respected. Franklin was like Derek, both men were honorable, even if

Franklin didn't want Tom dating Jess. He wondered if Derek felt the same.

I want to date your daughter. Tom reared back at the words begging to spill from his mouth. He lowered his gaze, and concentrated on eating, on not exposing any more of his heart other than what these two good people had already seen. He wouldn't take advantage of this situation, or exploit it. He finished, complimented Leonie on the meal, then thanked them both for their hospitality.

"We're the ones who should be thanking you, Tom." Leonie's eyes shimmered. "She's got a loyal friend in you."

"I care about her," he said gruffly, then stood and rinsed his bowl in the sink, like he would at his own family's home. He exhaled, willed his face to not wear his heart, and turned. "Well, I'll leave you to it." He clicked for Benji to come. "Please let me know...uh, how she does."

Leonie nodded. "We'll let you know how she gets on. Come here." She drew him down for a hug and patted his back. "She cares about you too. You'll see."

He had to blink hard against the emotion as he hugged her. "Thanks."

He held out a hand to Derek. "See you next time."

"Don't let it be so long, okay?"

Was this the acceptance he'd been searching for? Seemed like so. "Yes, sir."

Derek half-smiled. "It's Derek and Leonie, Son. I thought you knew that by now."

Leonie slapped his arm. "Stop teasing the young man. You know he's polite, and trying to get in your good books."

"Mrs. James—"

Her mouth curved. "You bringing our daughter here is exactly what gets you in our good books. Now we just need to convince that stubborn brother of hers that you should be in his good books too."

"Amen," he muttered without thinking.

Leonie's eyes gleamed. "I knew it."

Tom winced. "Okay, on that note, I'm definitely out of here. But please tell her I'm thinking about her. That I'm praying for her."

"We'll be sure to pass that on."

"Thanks." He put Benji back in his travel crate, and made the lonely trip through the dark back to his condo. So much had happened. And now, with what seemed to be her parents' blessing, even though they might not have said the specific words, once she was feeling better, so much had the potential to happen. Especially if Franklin could find it in his heart to agree.

His phone rang the next morning, Franklin's name lighting the screen. "What's this I hear about you and my sister?"

Tom yawned. "Good morning to you too."

He put the call to speaker and tapped open his messages. Saw one from Jess. His heart thudded, and he tapped it open. Two words.

Thank you.

She was probably too tired to write much more.

"Tom? Are you even listening to me?"

Right. Franklin. "Sorry, I just woke up."

"At this hour?"

"I had some trouble getting to sleep." Remembering what had happened. Realizing why it had. Imagining the worst. Like what he'd read about in that article about suicide rates among veterinarians. Jess's friend from college who had killed herself. He shivered.

"What happened?" Franklin asked.

"With what?" Franklin might be the one who grew up on a ranch, but Tom could play dumb until the cows came home.

"Last night. You and Jess. Mom posted something in our

family chat and asked us to pray for Jess, then when I called Mom she'd said she'd had some kind of mental breakdown."

Tom's heart dropped. *Lord, be with her.*

"She said you'd dropped Jess home last night," Franklin continued. "Why were you with her? Haven't I told you not to date her?"

Tom fought frustration and sought to speak evenly. "It wasn't a date." He explained as best he could. "I took her to your parents' and they were grateful."

Franklin was quiet for a long moment. "She's been stressed for months."

"I know."

"How do you know?"

"Because we're friends. And friends talk to each other, and I've seen that she's been struggling."

"Why didn't you say anything?"

"Because of this. You don't seem to want me to even talk to her, which is dumb. It's not like I'm a bad dude. I would've thought you would want someone you know to be your sister's friend."

"That's all you are?"

"Yes." At the moment, anyway. If she changed her mind, then he was three thousand percent here for that. Not that he'd say that right now.

"I just didn't want things to get complicated."

"Can't you see it's already complicated? And the only one who has complicated things is you."

Franklin was silent for a beat. Two. Then, "Mom said she's pretty sick."

"I think she's worn down mentally and physically. Your mom is concerned that Jess doesn't seem to have been eating well." Like when she didn't finish her taco. "But she's with your folks now, so hopefully that will help her eat better and find some peace."

"Hmph."

"'Kay, well it's been great to talk." Sarcasm wasn't his go-to, but it suited right now. "Say hi to Hannah for me."

"Hey—"

He stabbed his phone to end the call. Maybe it was petty of him, but he really didn't want to be talking to Franklin when he'd much rather be talking to Franklin's sister.

He found his message from her again. Tapped out a reply:

You're welcome. I've been praying for you 🙏

Moments later her reply came:

He exhaled heavily. Objectively, he knew a heart was a simple way to respond when a person didn't have the words. And he suspected Jess didn't have too many words right now.

But subjectively, he knew that a red heart symbolized a lot more. And that Jessica James had never been the kind of girl to fill her communications with emojis. So was her mom right and Jess did perhaps care for him? A little bit, at least?

He plunged his face in his hands, staring at the phone. This was way too much for him to think about so early in the day, even if it was nearly nine.

He slumped back against the padded bedhead, and flicked open his Bible app. Rather than wonder about what message Jess might or might not be sending, he'd be better off filling his mind with things that were true, were good and right. So he read 1 Corinthians 13 and prayed instead.

WEARINESS CLUTCHED AT HER. She opened her eyes. Closed them. Too much light. Her thoughts seemed to have drifts of coherency then long tracts of nothing. She was fairly sure she hadn't just dreamed that Tom had held her last night. That he'd lifted her and placed her in bed. Had he kissed her goodnight? Or had she dreamed that part? Tom was like a dream, a mist, a fog. Nothing felt too fixed or firm where he was concerned.

She reached for her phone. Tapped it open. Saw a long list of missed calls. Tension rose, pounding in her heart, behind her eyes. *You're a failure, failure, failure.* Far from being the smart person she'd always thought herself, she'd proved just how far she'd fallen short. She couldn't do it. Couldn't do it. Everything—work, life —was too hard.

She closed her eyes, and might've slept a few minutes, a few hours, she didn't know. When next she woke, light streamed from the window, so it was daylight still. Why was she here at her old bedroom? Wasn't that part of the dream?

Her side ached, her head throbbed, her heart was sore. She rolled over, uncertain what was real and what was her imagination. Tom had been there in her dream again, holding her, hugging her, whispering words she now wished she could remember.

A shiver rippled through her. So cold. Too cold. She reached out to the bedside table. Grasped her phone. Ignored the missed calls. Saw she had several new text messages. Including—her heart thudded—one from Tom.

> You're in my prayers.

In the wintry bleakness that was her internal existence, his words were like a fire on a snowy day, warming her heart. She liked to be in his prayers. Liked to know he thought about her. She wanted him to think about her. Wanted him to care. He was a good guy. A good, handsome guy. Strong, fit, kind, compassionate, growing in Christlike qualities, everything she liked in a man.

Her eyes drifted closed, her heart growing tender, thinking on him. Such a nice guy. He hadn't even seemed to mind the fact she'd wrecked his t-shirt, snotting on him the way she had, falling apart the way she had. Ugh. She shivered again, this time in embarrassment. Not that he'd been embarrassed. God bless him, he'd been kind. Kind Tom. Nice Tom. Sweet Tom. It was a shame that Franklin didn't want her dating any of his teammates. Well, too bad. If Tom was to ask, she might just say yes.

She drifted off to sleep and dreamed of Tom's lips in her hair.

When next she awoke it was to a heavy head and weighted, sticky eyelids. When she pried them apart—eye gunk from too many tears was so not cool—she saw her mom sitting in the chair beside her bed. "Mom."

"Oh, honey. You're finally awake." Her mother brushed Jess's hair from her brow. "How are you feeling?"

She yawned. "A little bit better."

"You've been really tired, haven't you?"

"Exhausted," she admitted.

"They've been working you so hard at the clinic."

The clinic? Oh no! Work! Heart hammering, she wearily pushed upright. "I'm late."

"No. You're not going to work today. You're sick, remember?"

Sick of work, a little voice whispered. "But if I don't go, I'll lose my job." She glanced around. Why was she here at the ranch? "Where are my work clothes? I need to get back—"

"Jess, you need to rest. Your clothes are in the wash. Work survived without you yesterday, they can survive another day, too."

"I've already missed one day?"

"You were asleep, honey."

Fresh regrets roared, sparking tears. She'd failed. She had responsibilities she couldn't keep. She'd failed Lisette. Failed work. Always such a failure...

So she sank back against the pillows, closed her eyes against the tears, and sank under the weight of sorrow and sleep.

NINE

The next few weeks passed in a welter of delays, like Tom's life was on hold. He might be doing the normal things, taking Benji for runs, talking with his family and friends, avoiding the tourists in town for the Calgary Stampede. But he still felt a little lost, like a kid searching for a missing puzzle piece, or trying to find the way home, walking around in circles in an endless waiting game. Waiting for Leonie to call with another update. Waiting for Jess to respond to his latest text. Waiting for Franklin to return, so he could visit and 'accidentally' glean what he could about Jess's condition.

Leonie had messaged him once to say Jess was sleeping a lot, and was keeping her phone usage to a minimum. That explained Jess's lack of response, but his heart felt sore. He didn't want to harass Leonie for more details, even though thoughts of Jess began and closed his days.

She hadn't returned to the clinic. He'd received a message to say the dog training had been postponed indefinitely, that 'due to unforeseen circumstances, Dr. James was taking an indefinite leave of absence.'

Unforeseen? Anyone with two eyes could have seen the soul-crushing weight of responsibilities was just too much. He hoped that the phrase 'indefinite leave of absence' meant she'd quit.

But it might just mean she was too sick or too sad to make such a momentous decision, or that she was catching up on a life-time of necessary sleep.

Whatever it meant, he should pray for her. So he prayed for her to know peace. Prayed for her comfort. Prayed she'd find rest, true rest, for her mind, her body, and her soul. And as he prayed his heart grew even softer, more tender towards her, his feelings strengthening into deeper affection, until he felt they were getting pretty close to love.

July slipped into August, which meant ramping up his training. Training camp was in the middle of September; the end of September would see the first pre-season games. And while his contract pretty much assured him a place on the team he still felt a measure of wanting to prove himself worthy.

He occasionally texted Jess, but received no answer. Leonie had mentioned Jess was off her phone, but he wished she'd jump back on it for him.

Franklin had returned, and he joined him and Hannah, Mike and Bree Vaughan at Mike's house, enjoying the pool after a hot summer's day. As the wife of the team's captain, Bree's hospitality was legendary, even if illness a couple of years ago meant she'd needed to tone down things a little in recent years.

"So, Tom, how has your summer been?" Bree asked, after Hannah and Franklin had shared about their highlight-reel of a trip in Italy.

"Nothing nearly as exciting." He drained his diet lemonade.

"Hmm, I seem to remember you had some nice pics of a lake," Mike said.

That felt so long ago. "It was good to go fishing, see my fami-ly." He knew Bree was fond of babies, so he mentioned Sadie's latest accomplishments that Michelle had recently shared. "She's pretty cute when she's smiling."

"Have you got a picture?" Bree asked. Then when he showed her, cooed, "Oh, she's adorable!"

Bree glanced at Mike but he shook his head. "No more babies, remember?"

She sighed. "I love children."

That explained why she had four.

She turned to Hannah, a mischievous glint in her eyes. "So, how about you two? Any plans for a baby James any time soon?"

Hannah blushed but shook her head. "We're happy to wait a few more years for that joy."

"Hmm." Bree looked at Tom. "And I suppose you need to find the right lady before we can have this conversation with you."

He half-smiled, but didn't answer. He'd found the right lady, but the fact that her over-protective brother sat two seats away drew reluctance to share the truth.

"I once thought you were sweet on Jess." Bree's purply-gray eyes gleamed with interest.

Heat flushed his neck, and he refused to look in Franklin's direction. Couldn't find the right words to reply, either. He wiped away the beads of condensation trickling down his glass.

Bree's glance swiveled between him and Franklin. "How is she?"

Franklin sighed, as Tom's heart beat faster. Finally, he could get some answers.

"She's not actually doing too well at the moment." Franklin's brow furrowed. "She's been overwhelmed with work, then a bunch of things have affected her mental health. She's at the ranch with Mom and Dad. Mom said Jess spends most of the time asleep."

His heart twisted. Poor Jess. He hadn't realized things were still that bad. He wished he could see her.

"I'm so sorry," Bree said. "She's a vet, isn't she?"

Franklin nodded. "She graduated just over two years ago, and her boss has made her do an insane amount of overtime. To be honest, I think he's a bully."

From what Tom knew, he agreed, "One hundred percent."

"Oh, poor thing." Compassion washed over Bree's features. "That must've been so hard to deal with. No wonder she's feeling depressed."

"Especially when you're new and trying your best to prove you deserve your job," he muttered.

Franklin eyed him. Tom shrugged, studied his glass. He wasn't about to apologize for paying attention.

"You sound like you've gotten to know her well," Bree said to Tom.

"I was doing dog training lessons with her for a while."

"You were? I didn't know you had a dog."

He explained about inheriting Benji, and the arrangement he'd made with his sister. "So it means I get to keep Benji with me."

"But what about when you go on long road trips?"

Yeah, that. This arrangement worked over summer, but probably wouldn't long-term. "I need to find someone who is happy to take on pets over those days."

"Maybe when Jess is better she can recommend one," Hannah offered.

Franklin didn't speak.

Bree seemed to notice, her gaze shooting between the others. "What's wrong, Franklin?" she asked. "Do you want Benji to live with you?"

"We couldn't have a dog," Hannah said, with an apologetic look at Tom. "Not in our apartment, and not when my work is so hectic."

"I'd offer," Bree said, "but we got Thumper for Ethan's birthday, and I'm not sure if I'm up for looking after two dogs and four children under six."

Mike shrugged an arm around her. "That's right, hon. You

need to be careful with your energy levels. You don't need to feel responsible for fixing everyone else's problems."

Tom shot her an assuring smile. He'd find a solution. *Please God.*

The conversation drifted to focus on Hannah's upcoming media projects, then moved to Poppy, Franklin's youngest sister, and her dancing career in Winnipeg.

Tom listened, picking at the plate of fruit Bree had set out. Poppy had always come across a little too assertive to him, and a little too much of a princess. He preferred someone more practical and compassionate, who might still possess dreams, but also had the gumption and grit to grind it out. His heart dipped. Except instead of grinding things out, it seemed that Jess had some of life ground out from her.

As Franklin and Mike discussed some of the other Northwest Ice guys they knew, Tom slumped in his seat, toying with the edges of the linen tablecloth. *Lord, please heal her, help her, give her strength.*

"What are you doing?" Hannah asked from beside him, a slight smile on her face, as the conversation swirled around them.

He shrugged. "Just praying."

Her eyes softened. "For a certain someone we both know and love?"

Heat scorched his cheeks. "I don't know about that last."

"Oh, I do. I saw the way you looked at her while you danced together at our wedding," she teased.

Man. How much had his face given his feelings away? Would he never live that down?

She studied him thoughtfully. "Hey, want to come with me to visit the ranch this weekend?"

"What? Why?"

"Poppy is back this weekend, so they're planning a barbecue and maybe a swim in the river. It'd do Jess good to see another friendly face."

"I couldn't."

"You could," she countered.

"It sounds like family only."

She smirked. "Well, I'm now family, and I'm happy to invite you."

"But I'm not." He nodded to Franklin. "And he's not a huge fan of mine."

"I think that's more because he's feeling a little guilty that you'd noticed what he hadn't. He takes his big brother duties seriously."

"You think?"

She chuckled, which drew the attention of the others. "What are you two talking about?" Franklin asked.

"I just invited Tom to come with me to see Jess this weekend." Hannah shot Tom a wink.

God bless her, but her husband didn't seem too pleased, judging from that frown. "Why?"

"Because he's her friend. And I think she'd appreciate a different face."

"And he does have a handsome face," Bree chimed in, throwing Tom her own good-natured wink.

Tom's neck heated as Mike rolled his eyes, like he was used to his wife's tease.

"Not that you're not handsome," Bree assured Mike. "Gosh, it's good to have a husband who is so secure that you can compliment another man, isn't it, Hannah?"

"Sure is." Hannah kissed Franklin's cheek. "This one is so secure and loves his family *so* much he'd do anything to help them, wouldn't you honey?"

Franklin sighed, then looked at Tom. "Fine. You can come."

His heart thudded. To finally get the chance to see Jess again? He'd take it. "Thanks."

"You should bring Benji, too," Hannah said. "I bet she'd love that."

Good idea. Benji might be one of those keys to helping heal a certain vet's heart.

"COME *ON*, JESS." Poppy bounced up and down on her bed like a five-year-old. "You should make an effort." Her nose wrinkled. "At least make enough effort to have a shower. Your hair is pretty gross and greasy."

Irritation flared, and she clamped her lips together. Any second now her pesky younger sister would go, and she'd be free to wallow in her misery again.

"Hey, don't hassle her," Cassie, their eldest sister said from the door. "You know Mom said she needs to take it easy."

"But it's a beautiful day, and the water might actually be warm by now. Or at least not feel like it's straight from a glacier." Poppy glanced at Cassie. "Remember how much fun we had at Hannah's bachelorette day?"

Fragments of memory merged together from just over a year ago. Jess had helped Cassie organize a day for Hannah and her friends by the river, followed by movies and high tea at the farmhouse. And while it might've been a special occasion before Hannah's wedding with Franklin, it had also marked the start of Cassie's own romance with Harrison Woods, the actor of *As the Heart Draws*, the historical drama that filmed in Three Creek Ranch's very own western town. The drama of the day had only been heightened by Harrison's unfortunate incident with a snake. Her heart prickled, remembering her own heroics, before moroseness stole in again. The strong, decisive Jess of a year ago seemed so far away from who she was today.

But... maybe Poppy was right and Jess should make more of an effort. It would do her good to get some sunshine on her face. Spending as much time as she had in this bed was making her back sore.

Yet the thought of having to interact, to play pretend with Poppy and Harrison and Hannah and the others was exhausting. And if just the thought of seeing them exhausted her, then actually seeing and speaking to them was sure to be a hundred times worse.

"I'm sorry Poppy, but I think I'd rather stay here."

"But you'd have fun. I *know* it."

Fun felt like a concept for other girls. She might not be working at that cesspit of a job, but smiling, laughing, felt like a foreign language she couldn't speak. Had she ever? Well, she had with some people. Her lips pressed together. Some people had brought it out of her.

As Poppy departed, Jess's eyes blurred with the too-easy tears that sprang to life these days. Oh, she wished she could be normal, didn't have this depression or whatever it was that she'd overheard Poppy whisper. Was this feeling of emptiness and lethargy depression? Mom called it exhaustion. Dad said she needed time. They'd all prayed with her.

Christians weren't supposed to get depressed, were they? It was hardly living the victorious life of Jesus to feel this way, like a slug, unable to move, unable to see bright points in her day. She'd thought Poppy's return might spark some joy, but honestly, she was kind of exhausting. Her relentless positivity just highlighted Jess's lack of any. Even Cassie seemed to have a happiness and peace Jess envied, despite the challenges surrounding the *As The Heart Draws* production. All of her siblings were forging ahead, living their best lives, while she had proved she couldn't handle life at all. Hence she was stuck here, waiting, wondering how long she'd stay helpless like this.

"Honey?" Her mom tapped on the open door, then came in. "Poppy said you wanted to stay home."

She nodded, even if she wondered if that was true. "I'm too tired."

Disappointment swept across her mom's face. "I'd hoped you might like to come."

See? She was a bad daughter as well as a bad friend. But the regrets wouldn't change her mind. She didn't like the feeling of being managed, of having people plan her life, like they thought she was incapable of making any decisions. And just because that might actually be true didn't mean she wanted people thinking that.

Irritation flared. "I don't want to."

Her mom studied her a moment, then nodded.

Guilt pressed in. See? She was a bad daughter. Bad friend. Bad sister. The others were better off without her. They'd have more fun.

She turned and rolled away, her eyes brimming with fresh moisture, and listened as the rest of the household made their preparations for an afternoon at the river. Then let the tears spill, as woe gripped her, until exhaustion overcame her and she slept.

A FAINT CREAK stole to her ears, fluttering her lashes to lift. What—? Was somebody here? A click, click, click followed, then a soft voice, but she couldn't hear what they said.

It wasn't her family, that was for sure. Her family, who barged into her life and told her exactly what they thought. So who? A burglar? Somebody worse?

Fear pounded through her veins, and she pushed upright. Her bedroom's door was ajar, so they might come in here at any minute. And then do—what?

She slipped from the bed, suddenly conscious of her stained Minnie Mouse PJs, pimples and lank hair. She smelled bad too, exactly like the person she was who hadn't showered in a few days. Ugh. Still, her bad B.O. might be enough to deter an intruder. She'd likely pass out if she met someone who smelled like she did. She ran her tongue over her teeth. They were probably furry, too. Good. A twin combo of halitosis and B.O. should knock this prowler off their feet.

She inched to behind the door, picked up a tennis racquet she hadn't used in years, and waited, waited...

A tap on the door. "Jess?"

She frowned. Did she recognize that voice?

The door slowly pushed open.

How dare someone try to invade her space? She lifted the racquet, unused muscles protesting at holding it high for so long.

Then the door was suddenly shoved wide, and she caught a glimpse of a yellow Labrador as she swung the tennis racquet low and clobbered a man instead, spilling flowers over the floor.

The racquet slipped from her hands as she realized who it was.

Her hands covered her mouth. Oh no. *Oh no.*

"Tom!"

TEN

Tom rubbed his shoulder where the racquet had struck him. Then peered at the woman standing horrified just beyond. The one Benji was sniffing at.

She placed a hand on Benji's head, as if unconscious of the fact, her eyes still fixed on him. "Tom."

He smiled ruefully. "That wasn't exactly the welcome I was hoping for."

She seemed to crumple a little. "I'm so sorry. I didn't mean it."

"Yeah." He stretched out his arm. It worked. "It kinda felt like you did."

Tears trickled from her eyes and she swiped them away.

Regret at his joke made him step toward her. "Hey, I didn't mean—"

"Don't get any closer." She shrank back.

"Okay..." He moved back to the door. Saw how she relaxed. Like she thought him a scary dude. He, who had only ever tried to be her friend. His heart panged. "I'm sorry for scaring you."

"What are you doing here?" she whispered, her eyes huge.

"Hannah invited me. She thought you might like a visitor." His lips twisted. "Apparently not."

"No! No, I would, but—" She shook her head.

Benji, as if sensing her distress, shoved his face in her thigh. Her cute, PJ-clad thigh.

Tom blinked, bent and scooped up the flowers he'd spilled. "I'm really sorry for bothering you," he said gruffly. "I'll let you get back to sleep."

Her lips pressed together, and she shook her head.

What did that mean? He knew he wasn't as smart as her, but he didn't want to misread things. He'd already proved today that he was the top dog at getting things wrong. Why had he let Hannah talk him into this?

He knew why. Because he was a sucker for this woman, even if she hit him, and looked scared, and hadn't given him a single smile. Looked like he was the fool here.

"I'll go. Come on, Benji." He clicked, and Benji whined then obeyed, joining him as he retreated to the top of the stairs. His stomach wrenched with regret, with loss. Wow. What a mistake this had been.

"Tom, wait."

He peered back.

She stood in the doorway now. She wiped her face. "Give me a moment."

"Uh, sure."

She slammed the door, and he slowly trudged down the steps, Benji looking up at him inquisitively. He ruffled his head. "I don't understand, either."

Downstairs, he studied old black and white photographs lining the hallway that showed the progression of Three Creek Ranch from pioneer days to current times, with a photograph showing the family at last year's wedding.

He winced. What would Derek—and Franklin!—say if they knew he'd gone into her room? They'd likely want to hit him with more than a tennis racket. Franklin would likely want to slapshot him from here to Timbuktu.

Sounds of water running upstairs suggested she might be having a shower. "Don't think about that," he muttered. "Don't think about that."

"Don't think about what?"

He spun around and saw Franklin. Great. Here went nothing. "Um, nothing."

"Sure didn't sound like nothing to me." Franklin frowned. "What are you doing here, anyway? I thought you knew to join us at the river."

"I, uh, wanted to see Jess first. Your mom was here when I arrived and said I could go up. I wanted to give her these." He held up the battered looking bouquet.

Franklin looked askance at the floral arrangement.

"They looked better when I bought them," he defended.

"Did you drop them?"

"You could say that," he muttered. "Why are you here, if everyone else is at the river?"

"Dad asked me to get more ice. I saw your car and figured you must be here." He glanced up towards the stairs. "Is that the shower?"

"Jess said she'd be a minute," he mumbled.

Franklin's eyes widened. "She's getting dressed?"

That really didn't bear thinking about. "I don't know. But she asked me to wait."

"Wow." Franklin rubbed his chin. "Okay. Well, don't do anything I wouldn't do."

Was that acceptance, at last?

He nodded, and Franklin dipped his chin. "Want some help?"

Franklin shrugged. "Sure."

Tom followed him to the pantry off the kitchen, then helped him fill two coolers with ice from twin chest-high freezers, then Franklin left.

Tom exhaled. Benji whined, his tail wagging, as he hurried back up to the top of the stairs.

Where Jess stood. With just-washed hair, judging from the tiny rivulets dampening her sundress. She stood, her gaze uncertain, as Benji demanded she pay him attention by pushing into her bare legs. But Tom wasn't going to be outplayed by his dog. Not again.

"Hey Jess." He smiled.

"Oh Tom."

And she rushed at him and hurled herself against his chest.

He didn't know how long he hugged her. Time seemed to seep into minutes, maybe hours. He didn't know, didn't care. Only knew that this fresh-smelling, damp-haired woman fit snugly in his arms, like she was made to fit there.

"I'm so sorry," she whispered against his chest.

He rested his chin on top of her wet crown. "It's okay. I think it's good you know how to defend yourself."

Her breath caught on a broken laugh.

He'd take that as a win. "I'm just glad you spared poor Benji."

"Oh, poor Benji." She slid from his arms and crouched to finally give his ecstatic dog the attention he'd been hungering for. "I missed you, buddy."

Shoot. Outmaneuvered by his dog again. Still, he had flowers, bedraggled as they were. "I got you these."

She peeked up, and slowly rose, touching the peony whose petals were a little smushed. "You didn't have to."

"If I'd known you'd rather have a tennis ball then I would've bought one of those. Then you and Benji could have hours of fun together."

She peered at him quickly, like she'd heard the jealousy underlying his tone. He hadn't done a good job of hiding that. "Tom."

"Jess."

Her bottom lip quivered, and he realized afresh just how fragile she was still. She wasn't the woman he'd always been able to joke with. She might wield a racket with some force but her emotions ran super close to the surface. He swallowed a sigh. He'd messed up again. "How are you doing?"

She shook her head. "I don't know. Some days I don't even know who I am anymore."

"Hey, come here."

She stepped into his open arms and let him hug her again, then finally wrapped her arms around his back. "I'm really sorry about before. I didn't know you were here."

"It's all good. Nothing's broken. You'll have to try harder next time."

She pressed a little closer. "There won't be a next time," she murmured.

He pulled back. Did she mean—?

Her smile was uneven. "Don't look like that. I just mean I'm not in the habit of hitting men with sports equipment."

Thank goodness. He didn't want her to know her comment had scared him, so he made a joke. "Unlike some of us, huh?"

Her lips curved. "You get paid to do that."

He studied her, searching her eyes. "Are you okay?"

"I don't know. I'd like to say yes, but I feel like that's a lie."

"I don't want you to ever feel like you should lie to me. I care about you, Jess. You know that."

"I do." She ducked her head.

"I'm your friend."

She sucked in a shuddering breath. "I know." Then she hugged him again.

The bliss of this moment was stolen as Benji barked, and Tom grew aware of noise outside that suggested the return of an ATV. "Um, someone's here." He didn't want her embarrassed, or have to face any embarrassing questions himself.

"I don't care," she murmured.

Okay, then. He held on, pivoting slightly as the front door opened and Poppy appeared.

Poppy's mouth fell open. She met his gaze, emitted a squeak, then covered her mouth as Jess turned in his arms.

Then she rushed to take his place, clasping Jess in a hug and squeezing her tight. Her face peeked over Jess's shoulder and she mouthed a "thank you."

He smiled wryly, then shoved a hand through his hair, waiting for the two sisters to finish their bonding time. Okay, so judging from what he'd seen before, this wasn't Jess's normal.

"Oh, Jess. You look—and smell—so much better," Poppy said.

"Poppy!" Jess's cheeks flushed.

Tom bit his lip, and prayed desperately to not laugh.

"Look, we all know it's true. I bet even Tom does."

Wow. If he'd thought Jess a straight shooter, then Poppy was ten times worse.

Poppy flashed him a smile. "But I'm going to guess he's too much of a gentleman to say anything."

"I got nothing to say."

"Wise man." Poppy winked at him.

He glanced at where Jess was rubbing Benji's belly, his dog once again demanding her attention.

"It's good to see you, too," Jess murmured.

"You've made an impression," he said.

"She does that. On the right guys, obviously." Poppy winked again.

Now he could feel the embarrassment washing over his cheeks.

"At least you're not lying on the ground demanding your belly get rubbed."

"Poppy!"

He chuckled.

"What are you doing here, anyway?" Jess asked her sister.

"Franklin mentioned Tom was here," she motioned to Tom, "and that he'd thought you were finally joining the land of the living, so I came to make sure. And he was right!" She held up Jess's arm, in a victory pose. "You are!"

"I was glad to see him," Jess mumbled.

Heat glowed in his chest. That was more like it.

"Okay, well, no excuses now. You both need to come to the river. We need to have a party and celebrate the fact that Jess is finally out of bed."

"Poppy—"

"No, don't you go giving me any more excuses. Go back upstairs and put your bikini on. I bet Tom would like to see it."

"Poppy!"

He laughed. "Your sister is something else, isn't she?" he said to Jess. "I don't mind what you wear. But it's hot, so I wouldn't mind a swim if that's okay."

She glanced up at him. "I can come for a little while."

"As long as you want. I'll be right by your side."

SUNSHINE FELT strange on her skin after so long inside. But there was something special about seeing her family's faces of shock and joy, feeling their hugs of love, like they'd wanted her to make the effort that Poppy had demanded.

And to see Tom standing there, talking with Franklin and Harrison, like he just fit in, made the heat on her skin sink a little deeper. Of course, the fact he was bare-chested, thanks to an earlier dip in the river which meant she had full access to appreciating his tanned skin, might've sparked further awareness to her heart.

But she couldn't cope with Poppy's tease, or Cassie's smirks, or even Hannah's well-intentioned remarks. "He's nice but we're only friends," she insisted.

"Yet he's the only one who can inspire this Lazarus-like resurrection from the tomb." Poppy poked her.

Jess poked her back. "Stop it."

"I don't think I can." Poppy's face held unholy glee.

She glanced at Cassie. "Whatever happened to that guy Poppy was once sweet on?"

"Ooh, now this sounds like a good story," Hannah said. "Why don't I know about this?" She glanced at Poppy expectantly.

Sure enough, Poppy had quietened. "It's nothing. Nobody for you to worry about."

"What was his name?" Cassie asked. "Jack? John?"

A memory flashed. "Jake, wasn't it?"

"Jake the snake. *Not* anyone I ever want to think about," Poppy said firmly. "Especially not when a most beloved sister is finally out of the doldrums and is here with a handsome man who is begging for her to pay him attention."

"Poppy, don't! He'll hear you."

"Then he should put that chest away. It's not fair to the other guys here. No offence, ladies."

Cassie shoved her. "I happen to think Harrison is just as good looking as Tom."

"Just as?" Poppy arched a brow.

"Better!" Cassie snapped.

"And I wouldn't dare say any man is better looking than my husband," Hannah said.

"Wise words."

But for all the silly talk, Jess felt rather shy. It was one thing to joke about this, but these kinds of jokes felt like prodding a raw wound. She and Tom weren't together. She hadn't seen the man in weeks. And he'd been clear that she was his friend, nothing more.

She ducked her head, tears rushing back, like her tear ducts knew it had been too long since they'd functioned. Why had she hit him? Why couldn't she have behaved like a normal person, instead of this awkwardness where she felt like she had to tiptoe through life?

Just because she'd made it outside, and was with her family, didn't mean she would make a habit of this. She wasn't normal in that regard. This was a momentary aberration, that was all. She might've tried to grasp at feeling normal, but strong Jess was nowhere to be seen. Not anymore.

"Jess?" Cassie nudged her. "What's wrong?"

"I... I feel pretty tired." She yawned to emphasize it.

"Do you want to go back?" Hannah asked. Poppy watched her, arms folded.

"I think so."

"Stay a little longer. Please?" Cassie begged.

A cloud went over the sun, and it felt like one went over her heart too. "I can't."

"Jess, don't do this."

She shrugged away from Poppy's claw, and moved back towards the hill.

"Jess?" Mom hurried to her. "Are you okay?"

"No. I thought I could, but I just can't."

"But Tom—"

"Tell him I'm sorry."

Embarrassment lit her cheeks at the memory of how she'd clung to him earlier, like some needy, greedy child offered her favorite play-thing. Oh, she'd embarrassed herself *so* much.

She glanced up, saw he'd stilled, his eyes on her. His eyebrows rose, a silent question.

She shook her head.

He strode towards her, ignoring Franklin who was still talking. "Jess? Did you want to go back?"

She nodded, unable to speak, as a wave of emotion threatened her composure.

"I can take you if you like."

"Y-you should stay. Eat something."

"Jess, I'm not—"

"Tom, would you take her back?" her mom asked.

Great. So her entire family was conspiring against her? "I can manage, Mom."

"I'd feel better if Tom was to take you."

"I'm happy to." He shrugged on his shirt, picked up his towel and hat, and shook hands with Harrison, Franklin, and her father, before making a round of cheek kisses with the women. Poppy didn't settle for a kiss, throwing herself at him in a hug.

Her chest heated at Poppy's brazenness, but Tom only patted her back and drew away, his gaze returning to Jess. She lowered her head, as envy spiked at her sisters and mom receiving what she wanted, then wondering what his lips would feel like on hers. Her stomach fluttered. Then she shivered. Rubbed her eyes. This was madness.

"Are you okay?" he asked softly, clicking for Benji to join them in his vehicle.

"I don't know if I'll ever feel completely okay again."

"Little steps by little steps." He opened the passenger door, waiting as she got in. "You know everyone is happy to see you manage what you can."

Manage what she could? Her energy levels were dropping fast, proving she couldn't manage much at all. How could she have ever worked such long hours before? She sighed as he got in and shut the door. "I wish I knew who I was and what I'm supposed to do."

His hand covered hers. "You're a daughter of the Most High God. That's a good start, don't you think?"

Her eyes blurred, and she blinked back more tears, turning her head to peer out the window as he started the vehicle and slowly negotiated the road home.

The track was more a suggestion these days, even though it had been graded in previous years. Last year's filming at the river of some pivotal *As the Heart Draws* scenes that had seen Cassie score a cameo had not been repeated this year. Apparently river scenes—complete with angry garter snakes—were a risk too far for a TV production still reeling from the fact that Ainsley Beckett, their heroine since the show's inception, had declined from taking part in upcoming seasons.

She propped her head in her hands, as she thought about Ainsley. She'd managed to pivot from one very structured career focus to take a slightly different, broader path. Maybe Jess couldn't be a vet anymore. If so, then what did God have in store for her?

Tom was right. She was a child of God. She'd been leaving Him out of the picture for far too long.

Fresh tears leaked from under her closed eyelids. *I'm sorry God. I need You.*

"Hey." Tom slowed the vehicle, and she peeked to see they'd reached the house. He turned off the ignition, then placed his hand on hers. "It's okay. You don't have to have all the answers. God has got you in the palm of His hand."

Breath shuddered out. "How do you always know the right thing to say?"

He gave her a twisted smile. "I care about you. You're my friend."

That's right. If nothing else, she had God, a family who loved her.

And Tom. Her heart panged. Her friend.

Eleven

People underestimated the power of a hug. Well, maybe not the kinds of hugs exchanged between family members, but definitely hugs between friends of the opposite sex. Because Tom's experience of hugging his mom or sister or teammates was nothing compared to what he'd shared with Jess. He hadn't been able to forget the hugs they'd exchanged at the ranch. Three hugs before the river, then an extra long one when he'd dropped her home, when she'd whispered a "Thank you" against his throat.

He'd taken that caress of her breath against his skin to sleep that night, then had to wrestle with his dreams, and ask God to tamp down his imagination. Those hugs were powerful, her softness against his strength inducing the desire for more. A feeling only exacerbated when she'd enjoyed a brief swim. Not in the bikini Poppy had teased, but a plain black one piece that still stole his breath and forced him to school his features and concentrate on the fact her father and brother were mere meters away.

Even in this fragile state she was beautiful to him. Her paleness he attributed to time indoors, and the fineness of her features seemed exacerbated by her lost weight and the shadows under her eyes. Yet the fact she'd joined the others was surely progress, and well deserving of the party Poppy had declared it. Even if the days since had shown that two steps forward had also seen one step back.

He'd found out when he messaged her the next day and didn't get a reply, only learning from Franklin after training the following day that she'd spent the day in bed.

"It was great to see her finally leave her room, but it exhausted her," Franklin had said.

Tom understood. Socializing could be exhausting at the best of times, and it must be doubly so when she'd been used to keeping company with just her thoughts. But he knew—only too well—how being alone could play tricks on his mind, make him question what had been said and second guess himself. Had he somehow implied she did smell, like Poppy said? That woman really had a lot to answer for.

But he couldn't blame Poppy, when his own actions and imagination meant he was only too willing to get carried away himself.

Jess might've hugged him, and been embarrassed about some of her sister's pointed remarks about him, but it didn't mean that she wanted more. Maybe she'd been embarrassed because she simply didn't want more. That she saw him as only a friend, just like he'd hastened to assure. Had that been the right thing to say when he wanted more? Whatever. He would keep following those little heart promptings he thought might be Holy Spirit led, and do his best to be her friend.

How do you know it's spring time in Toronto?

How?

The Leafs are out.

He'd count that as a win. Then tried another one:

> What does a hockey player do on a beach
> holiday?
>
> ?
>
> Wayne Jetski.

No more response. Which was fair.
He tried again.

> How do hockey players stay cool during a
> game? They have lots of fans.
>
> :/

And yeah, that last one especially was bad, definitely earning that reaction. But he hoped that sending her a daily joke, something he hoped made her smile, brightened her day, just as her responses did his.

August slid into September, but since that time at the ranch reconnecting with Jess it seemed the days were brighter. Although 'connecting' felt like an overstatement. Their connection felt tenuous, at best. She might've opened the door to renewed communication but he wasn't going to push his way into demanding her attention. She was still fragile, and he was developing yet more patience, asking God for wisdom for how to bless her. Which meant sending her something each day, whether it be a joke or cartoon, Bible verse or picture of something he found good or lovely, just like the list of things outlined to think about in Philippians 4.

He didn't want to overwhelm her, but neither did he want her to think he'd forgotten her either. The days he received a reply, even if it was only an emoji, meant at least she was still communicating with him. A win.

On the days she didn't respond he figured she could simply

do with more praying. And as he prayed, she became even more entwined within his heart.

And it wasn't just silly jokes. He sent her Bible verses too. Like Philippians 4.13: "I can do all things through Christ who strengthens me." Or the verse in Proverbs 18 that said "The name of the Lord is a strong tower. The righteous run to it and are kept safe."

Anything encouraging, anything that let her know she was in his thoughts. Even pics of Benji.

"Look what Benji did when I mentioned your name." Yesterday, he'd sent a photo of Benji smiling, in one of those smiling dog pictures that could go viral on Instagram.

She'd sent a hearts eyes emoji back, something that made him wonder if she liked his dog more than him. Fair enough if it was so, because Benji was basically furry sunshine, while Tom definitely had his less sunshiney moments. Like when impatience bit, and he wondered how long it would be until they could actually have a real conversation, and he could learn the truth about why she'd collapsed....

He'd picked up snippets from the conversations he'd had on that day by the river with Leonie and Derek and Cassie. Things that suggested her collapse had been triggered by her friend's death, and the pressure of her work became too much, just as he'd suspected. She'd seen a doctor, and a therapist, who had prescribed an indefinite leave of absence from work, while she found her feet again.

No wonder she was feeling lost, not knowing who she was or what she was about. That was the problem with having workaholic tendencies. One could get lost in the work and find one's identity there rather than take that necessary step back and remember God was the Ultimate Creator, not a boss or a degree. Which left him praying for her to find who she was in God, for her to remember God held her in the palm of His hand, just as he'd said.

And it was equally important for him to know the same.

"Hello, love."

Jess accepted her mom's soft kiss on her cheek and slumped down in the chair at the kitchen table. Some days the energy it took walking from her bedroom downstairs was enough to tire her all day, leaving her longing for sleep.

But the therapist had said she needed to create some good routines, which meant no more days spent lingering in bed. It was like Tom's unexpected visit had shocked her into realizing just what she'd become. How embarrassing that he might've thought she smelled!

She ate breakfast—another daily habit she forced herself to do, even if she often wasn't hungry. But her ribs were kind of prominent, and she'd gone down a cup size, which wasn't great. Especially when she'd caught a glimpse of how Tom had looked at her when she'd finally taken off her sundress at the river, before he'd hastily averted his gaze.

This thing between them felt shaky, like she didn't know if she should settle for friendship like he seemed to want, or pursue more. But what was the point in wanting more when she wasn't herself yet? How did one have a define the relationship talk, when some days she was barely strong enough to tap out much of a response than an emoji?

"So, honey, what are you going to do today?" Mom asked.

She shrugged. "I don't know."

"You could go see Cassie. She's at the western town with Harrison."

"Mm, no thanks." She blinked, her mind felt fuzzy often these days. "What... what are you doing today?"

"I'd planned to make jam. You're welcome to help me. We've got to pick the fruit first."

Memories flashed of when she and her sisters used to help in the garden as little kids. Franklin and sometimes Cassie would help Dad fix fences, while Mom had asked Poppy and Jess to help in the kitchen. And while Jess had often wanted to check on the animals, she'd enjoyed making jam too, especially when it involved eating the cooled skins of sugared fruit puree that Mom said would rot their teeth. Good memories. Simpler times. "I... okay."

Her mom beamed, like Jess was the big girl she was proud of from two decades ago. A lump formed in her throat. Even if it felt ridiculous to take pride in something as silly and trivial as making jam.

Her phone buzzed, and she glanced down at an incoming picture. Her phone was safer to use now. Dr. Theo had been blocked from her phone, along with all the others from the clinic. Paige had sent a few messages, Denise too, but then paranoid her had started wondering if they were feeding her answers back to Dr. Theo and implying she was better and ready to resume work. She wasn't. She never wanted to work there again. But severing that connection by sending in a resignation letter still seemed a step too far. She was counting on her doctor and therapist's letters to extend her leave of absence for a little while longer.

This picture was from Poppy. A picture of her little girls dressed in pink tutus at her friend Bailey's ballet school in Winnipeg. Her lips lifted, but sweet as they were, they weren't as cute as some of the pictures someone else sent.

She scrolled through to his last message. He hadn't yet sent a joke today. Did he know she hung onto his words like they were gold? That each day was filled with anticipation about what he'd send? Most of his jokes were pretty corny, but showed he'd be ready to be the perfect dad one day.

His Bible verse encouragements fueled hope. And his pics of Benji made her heart both smile and grow sore. She wished Buster was here. Wished she had a doggy companion for those days when all she wanted was a cuddle. And if she couldn't have Tom here for hugs on demand—and let's face it, why would he when he was busy and she was weird—then a furry companion like Buster or Benji would make a nice alternative. Miranda didn't count. She might be the farm cat, but she'd never been faithfully friendly. No, she wanted someone who didn't ask too many questions. Who knew she needed to hear a solid heartbeat. Who she could get lost in their warmth and their kindness...

"Jess?"

Her eyes flew open. Had she fallen asleep again? "Sorry, Mom. Did you say something?"

Her mother's smile held patience. "Are you ready to go pick strawberries?"

"Sure."

"You might want to put a hat on."

"Oh. Okay."

Some days felt like she was that child of her memories, learning and relearning things. It felt weird for someone who had battled Lisette for top honors for years at university. Her eyes filled, she paused, her hand stretched toward the row of pegs for her hat. Poor Lisette. Poor Monique. *Lord, be with her family.*

"Sweetheart?"

Mom's voice broke the moment, and she forced herself to pay attention. She remembered when her grandfather had had a stroke, the way he'd be a little too slow to answer sometimes. And while she hadn't had a stroke, it felt like all the knowledge—and grief—she'd crammed inside had clogged her brain.

She put on her hat, went outside, and enjoyed the feel of the sun on her skin as she slipped into the rhythms of yesteryear, lifted the protective wire, and plucked plump strawberries from the plants.

She slipped one into her mouth. An explosion of sweet goodness filled her mouth. "Yum."

Her mother glanced up from where she was harvesting on a different row. "Are you sure you're helping or simply helping yourself?" she teased.

"I forgot how good home grown tastes."

"Nothing beats it."

Home grown. Nothing beat it. That was true. She'd kind of forgotten that in recent years, too busy trying to be the best, scale the ladder, and be the success everyone had always said she was. Memories flickered. Her grandparents, beaming with pride at her many school awards. Mom and Dad, thrilled and thankful for her scholarships that had seen her placed in one of Canada's best veterinary schools. So many years of study and hard work... And look where she was now. Picking berries like a seasonal worker with no education. Oh, foolish, foolish pride. Look where it had got her.

She plucked slowly, her steps dragging, and realized she was only halfway down her row compared to Mom who had almost finished. Mom, whom she'd often been impatient with in the past because Jess had thought she lacked ambition. Guess the pursuit of ambition had proved the false god after all.

"How's it going there?" her mom asked.

"It's going. I'm going." Slowly.

Her mom nodded. "I'm going to take this bucket inside then get started on the blueberries. Are you okay to stay out here?"

She peered up at her mom.

Her mother smiled. "I'll take that look as a yes."

She continued, and a blur of orange signaled that Miranda had slunk her way near.

"Hello." She held out her hand, but Miranda refused to be stroked. Mom and Cassie loved her for her mousing abilities, but Jess had always thought she was an independent thing. A bit like her, perhaps. Too busy following her call to really make the effort to make friends.

Her heart pained. If only she'd taken more time for Lisette, maybe Lisette would still be here. She dropped to her knees, squashing one of the strawberry plants. "Lord, is this guilt ever going to get better?"

Her eyes blurred, and she blinked back tears. She'd cried so much in recent weeks, like she had years-worth of tears stored up that were begging to be released. And now they had permission to.

Oh, if only she was stronger like before.

What if I don't want you to be like before? she felt a tiny voice whisper.

She reared back. What? Surely God wanted her to be the success she used to be. The person who was the strong one, a helper, independent, capable.

"God?"

Miranda pounced, and moments later, dropped a mouse beside the bucket, her tail swishing in satisfaction.

"Yes, you're a clever thing." Jess stroked her head, then Miranda pointed her little nose in the air and paraded off, like she knew her work here was done.

"Such a proud kitty cat."

She sipped her water, then used a nearby garden spade to pick up the dead mouse and fling it far beyond the fruit and vegetable patch. She might love animals, but dead mice didn't need to be buried like some city folk might think. People who grew up on ranches understood that a dead mouse might make a hawk or kestrel happy, and continue the circle of life that this land needed. "Sorry, Miranda, but I don't want your prize."

Just like I don't want yours.

She shivered. The sun might be out, but that felt soul-rippling.

How often had she gone to God, offering her accomplishments and awards as little trophies, while inside she'd simply been building up her storehouse of pride?

Her success at school. Pride. Her career. Pride. Her ability to 'do it all.' Pride.

Pride, pride, pride. It was insidious. It was everywhere.

And just as she didn't need or want Miranda's accomplishment, neither did God need hers.

Tears rushed to her eyes. Stupid tears. Yet more.

How long had she considered herself extra special simply because of what she'd done?

God wasn't interested in her accomplishments or activity. He was interested in her heart. And her heart had been a long way from Him lately.

Who was she? Not a vet. That didn't define who she was. She wasn't even simply Derek and Leonie's daughter, or someone who loved animals.

You're a daughter of the Most High King.

Tom's voice rippled in remembrance. She closed her eyes, remembering what he'd said. She knew it wasn't right to use a person to prop up her identity. She was dangerously close to letting Tom do that for her. But he was right. She didn't need him, or her job, or her success to shape how she felt about herself. She needed to look to Jesus, the author and perfecter of her faith. The one who truly cared about her, more than anyone, Mom, Dad, Cassie, Poppy.

"God." She slumped in the dirt. "I need You. I've been so full of pride. *So* full of pride. Please forgive me. Cleanse me, take it out, and heal my heart. I've got nothing."

Except Me, that little voice softly said.

"I've got You," she murmured.

And God had her.

For just like Tom had also said, God had her in the palm of His hand.

Twelve

Mid-September training camp meant an uptick of work, the long days of wondering how to spend his summer now concluded by a strict regimen of training, gym work, and team events. The team's upcoming schedule was fixed, so routine was key, and everything in his life would be second to it.

Which he was fine about, except this year it felt like things had changed. One, because his heart still hungered for a woman who appeared to have returned to radio silence. Two, because this year he had Benji.

It wasn't fair to a dog to leave him at a boarding kennel for a week or more, which is what he'd have to do several times this season, or so the calendar and game schedule said. Sure, others might do that while they took vacations, but it didn't seem fair or what Michelle had expected when she had asked him to look after Benji.

Benji needed companionship, the opportunity to run, to explore. Being cooped up for most of the day in his condo wasn't exactly fun.

His thoughts strayed to Jess. She might know what to do. But he didn't want to impose, no matter what his sister might advise.

Michelle's latest phone call had been fun. "Come on, Tom. What are you waiting for? Call the woman."

"I want peace about this, not just to rush in," he'd admitted. "I don't want her to feel obliged to do something she doesn't want. She's had enough of that already." He'd briefly explained about the toll on Jess's mental and physical health her work had had.

"Poor thing," Michelle murmured. "I'll be praying for her."

"Thanks," he'd rasped.

"But who knows? Maybe she'd love to hear from you, you know, to give her something good to think about. Hoo boy. I can't believe I'm saying that about my baby brother."

"I can't believe it either," he owned.

She'd laughed. "You should at least call her. Come on. Stop being a wuss!"

But that sense of internal Holy Spirit-led restraint held him back. And that sense of not wanting to intrude kept him quiet. Michelle could call him all the names under the sun; he didn't want to push his way into Jess's space when she very likely still had healing to do.

He tried to talk to Mike about what to do about Benji one day after training. "What do you do about Thumper when you go away on road trips?"

"What do you mean? Bree and the kids look after him."

Oh, right. "Stupid question," he mumbled.

Mike's eyes widened. "Ah, Benji needs to be babysat, huh?" He winced. "I wish I could say Bree could—I know she could and *would*, one hundred percent, but I don't like to put more pressure on her. The twins are being little terrors at night, and I don't think we need to throw another dog in the mix. Sorry."

"It's okay. I'll figure something out."

Mike frowned. "I could ask my folks."

"Benji is really well-behaved. He knows how to behave indoors."

"Yeah," Mike winced. "My mom is not an indoor pet kind of person."

That was a wash-out then. Benji couldn't stay outside when the temperatures would be dropping into the minuses next month. "Thanks, anyway."

"So what are you going to do?" Mike asked.

He shrugged. "I guess I'll have to investigate boarding kennels and book in those dates right away."

"Or you could ask Franklin if his sister might know someone who'd like a pet dog occasionally."

His heart thudded. Would *Jess* like to look after Benji on a part-time basis?

No. That was dumb talk. She was probably still upset about losing her own pet, and not ready to consider a new one. Even if she would be the perfect person. Wouldn't she?

His gaze veered to Franklin. He didn't want to keep asking the man for intel on his sister. But when she wasn't answering his messages—not even with an emoji—he wasn't sure what to do.

"I don't know." *Lord?*

How long did God want him to be patient for? It felt like an eternity since he'd been at the river and seen her. Yet he'd sensed a caution in his spirit about calling her. Maybe he'd been a little too persistent in his daily reminders and she'd backed off. Whatever it was, he wasn't about to ask Franklin for advice.

He prayed about it for the rest of that day. Prayed about it when he played with Benji, and the big brown eyes looked up at him beseechingly. This dog had so much love to give. Benji deserved an owner who would care for him. *Lord, what is Your answer?*

SHE DIDN'T SHOW up during the pre-season fan sessions. Disappointment panged his heart when he searched the stands and she wasn't there. He lifted a hand to Cassie, Leonie and

Derek and they waved back. Then he realized they were waving at Franklin, behind him.

Cool. Loved making a fool of himself like that.

He skated closer to where his own parents sat. Mom beamed, Dad grinned, soaking in the atmosphere. Tom knew Dad hadn't been shy about boasting about his son playing in the NHL. Michelle and Travis were there with Sadie, at her very first game, complete with pink earmuffs.

They had skills sessions—fastest skater, hardest shot, most accurate shot—but the usual drive to show off wasn't there. Not when somebody else wasn't.

Later, after a scrimmage designed to look like a real game, he caught up with his family. And while he deeply appreciated the fact they'd driven for hours to come see him, his thoughts twisted to the woman who couldn't bother driving less than an hour. Not that he'd say that. Even if his sister kept eyeing him like she knew something was wrong.

Fortunately for him—unfortunately for her—Sadie started fussing and they had to make their apologies and leave.

"Sorry we can't hang longer." Travis leaned in for a man-hug.

Tom back-slapped him. "Thanks for coming, bro." His only brother. By marriage, but it counted. Franklin's big frame caught his eye. He angled to not see him.

"See you, Princess." He tickled Sadie's pink-clad toes. "Be good for Mommy, okay?"

Michelle passed Sadie to Travis and hugged Tom properly. He closed his eyes, remembering the last person who had fully encased him in a hug like this. The one who wasn't here.

"Hey, is everything okay?" Michelle murmured.

"All hunky dory."

Her brow pleated. "Are you sure? You seem a bit distracted." She pulled back. Glanced around, her gaze zeroing in on where Franklin and his family were talking. Her frown deepened. "Wait, she's not here, is she?"

No guesses for who she referred to. He could play dumb, or own the truth. "Nope."

"Why?"

"I haven't heard from her in weeks," he admitted.

"Oh, Tom." Her expression softened. "I didn't think she was the type to ghost someone."

He shrugged, shoved his hands in his pockets to give them something to do. "I haven't pushed because I think she's figuring stuff out." And he'd sensed that Holy Spirit caution to wait. "I'm praying for her."

"Of course." She nodded. "I'll continue to pray for her too. I imagine there must be a lot to have to contend with after an incident like that."

"Are we talking about Jessica?" Mom asked.

"Yeah. She's not here, which is why Tommy is sad."

"I'm not sad." He flicked his pesky sister.

She flicked him back. "What are we? Five?"

"Michelle, stop picking on your brother," Mom said.

"But he started it."

Mom wrapped an arm around his waist. "My son. You did well tonight. And you'll make the right choice about your lady friend."

His neck heated. "Mom."

"Just be patient. Give her time. She needs to heal."

"Yeah."

He hugged his parents, Dad once again telling him how proud he was of him, and they arranged to catch up for breakfast tomorrow morning.

"I need to see if Benji remembers me," Michelle said.

"I'm sure he will. You're not exactly easy to forget."

"Why thank you." She stuck her tongue out at him as if to prove the fact.

They left, and he talked with Bree and Ethan as they waited for Mike to finish his captain duties. He wondered how long it'd be until Mike retired. The man still played as well as ever, but there were times when he seemed to come alive with his family like he didn't do so much on the ice. He clearly adored his wife and kids.

His heart twisted, and he studied his shoes. Everyone here seemed to have someone. Even the newbies had a girlfriend clinging to their side. And he was here and the woman he wanted was not... Would she ever reconsider him as more than a part-time friend?

Someone touched his arm. Cassie. He shoved his morose feelings aside. "Hey, good to see you." He hugged her.

"You too."

"How have you been?"

He small-talked for a while, avoiding the topic closest to his heart. He felt strangely vulnerable and didn't want anyone poking at his wound. It felt poked enough already by his family's remarks.

He refocused on Cassie, on what concerned her. "So, *As The Heart Draws* has renewed for another season, huh? That's great."

"It definitely helps, but I guess it's showed the importance of expanding our thinking so we're not dependent on one main income source."

"You have the ranch accommodation, don't you?"

"The cabins on the western town lot, yes." Her head tilted. "But now you mention it, there are some empty farm buildings, way over near the southern boundary line. Maybe we could rent them out." Her forehead furrowed. "We would need to fix up the access road. I don't think anyone has been out that way in months."

"Probably best to make sure a bear hasn't moved in."

"If there's three, we'll just send in Goldilocks."

"Huh?" Then he caught the fairy tale reference. "Are you her?"

"No." A faint smile traced her face. "That'd be a certain vet we both know and love."

He shook his head. He knew she was teasing, but this up and down of emotion had him heart-sore.

"I'm sorry."

"It's okay."

"She's doing a lot better these days."

Except she still wasn't talking to him.

"Have you heard from her at all?"

"Not for a couple of weeks."

"Oh. Oh! That's probably when…" She bit her lip.

The polite thing to do would be to let that comment slide. He wasn't so polite. "When what?"

Her nose wrinkled. "She's been going through some things. But I think she's turned a corner. Just be patient."

"Sure." These days, patience seemed to be his middle name.

Cassie squeezed his arm. "Look, Jess isn't really a fan of big crowds yet. But you should come visit again."

His heart flicked. He tamped it down. "I don't want to intrude."

"You're not intruding. You've been invited."

But not by the person he wanted to invite him.

"Come on, Tom. Don't be stubborn. You know she'd like to see you."

"Actually, I don't know that. Which is why it'd be good to have her say something so me turning up isn't an unpleasant surprise."

"It wasn't an unpleasant surprise before, remember? She cares about you, Tom."

Be nice if she showed it. "My number hasn't changed if she wants to stay in touch."

"I'll remind her."

"Thanks." Gruffness filled his tone. He cleared his throat.

He didn't want to force himself into a situation where he'd be unwelcome. But neither was he going to close the door. The door was open, but it was up to her to walk through.

He wasn't about to force her hand.

JESS STROKED BELLE'S NOSE, her horse's heavy breath hot and oaty. "It's good to be with you." She'd missed Belle. Missed riding. She glanced around the pasture, dotted with Angus cattle, and drew in a deep breath scented with freshness. "It's been too long."

Just like it had been too long since she'd seen a certain someone else. But just because she might want to see someone didn't mean she should. And just as she hadn't been physically strong enough to sit atop a horse, neither had she been emotionally or spiritually strong enough to see Tom. She wanted to feel whole in God's sight, not use a man's affection to fill up her broken internal spaces.

She might yearn to see Tom again, but having him around was too distracting. It was too easy to let go of God and lose herself in something else instead. Or someone else, in this case.

So she'd backed off, retreated. Which probably was confusing as all heck for him, seeing she'd basically thrown herself at him the last time they were together. Oh, who was she kidding? She *had* thrown herself at him. Literally. And several times, too. Savored the feeling of safety in his arms. Known the assurance of his heart ticking steadily away.

Because that was the kind of guy Tom was. Not just a joker, he was steady. Strong. Good. A man of God, just like her dad, who had been a tower of strength in recent weeks. Someone she could turn to when life felt rocky.

She glanced at her dad now, seated astride while she rode Belle. He was studying one of the cows, a frown pleating his face.

Accompanying him on his rounds was usually Cassie's job, but she'd been asked by Mal Hendricks, the lead director for *As The Heart Draws* to stand in again for Brenda, the stuntwoman, who'd had to go to court today to take the stand against her violent ex-husband.

Lord, be with Brenda today.

Jess was trying to pray for others more often these days. People like Brenda, Monique, the other members of Lisette's family. She had to be outward looking, less in her own head. Negativity had a way of spiraling faster when she only focused on herself. But just like going to the river with Tom had been a breakthrough and hit pause on her self pity and grief, so accompanying her father on his rounds of the ranch had broken down a little more of the pain inside. Maintaining focus on others, maintaining connection with God, it all helped her ride those waves of pain that still threatened to swamp her.

The Lord is my strong tower, the righteous run to it and are safe.

She needed to remember that. Rather than trying to hide from God, or letting herself become so consumed by work or busyness or good things or good people like Tom, she needed to regularly run to God.

Mom had quoted from her Bible study something about how an orchestra needed to tune in to each other, to tune together to be in sync before they performed for the day. So also Jess needed to tune into God at the start of each day. And here, at the ranch, where each day began with a gentle stillness of dawn, she found herself embracing the cool as the sun slowly swept across the valleys.

God was here, ready and waiting each morning. And though she still felt a little frail, gradually the strength of His promises was proving—once again—that He was ever faithful. Ever dependable. Steady. Strong.

Just like someone else she knew.

"Lord, help me to stop thinking about him," she whispered.

But her traitorous mind refused to obey. Why hadn't he contacted her recently? Had he found someone new? She'd checked his Instagram—on her computer. She'd deleted all the social media from her phone, knowing it wasn't good for her head space to spend so much time mindlessly scrolling through her phone.

But he'd posted nothing recently—certainly no unbuttoned

shirt pics—apart from his excitement about the new hockey season beginning soon.

Regret twisted her stomach. She wished now she'd gone to see him at the Hockey Skills Day. Wished she'd had the courage to face the crowds and cheer him on. Wished she had the strength to resist him if he smiled at her. But because she didn't yet, she hadn't. Which left her wondering how he was, wondering if she could dare ask Cassie or Mom, or if that would give the game away.

"You're busy thinking."

She glanced at her father. "So are you. Are you worried about the cows?"

"I'm not worried. Just thought I'd see if the vet had any expert opinion."

"You know I'm more of a small animal specialist than a large one. But I'll have a look." She swung off Belle and hitched her to the post.

The cow's nose was red, raw from rubbing it to get rid of mucous discharge, the fever and conjunctivitis suggesting the highly contagious Infectious Bovine Rhinotracheitis was the culprit.

"I think she's got IBR, so we need to isolate her from the rest of the herd. Have you noticed the same symptoms in any of the others?"

"Nope."

Her father slid from his saddle and they spent the next hour checking and rechecking the cow herd, until they were both satisfied the problem was isolated to one. Dad gently lassoed her and brought her to the barn where a stall was set up as an isolation area.

Memories slipped in of when she'd done similar things in her training, remembering Lisette holding the front end while she'd been at the back, before a pile of steaming manure was deposited on her shoe. Lisette had always been smarter than her.

Her eyes stung, and she blinked emotion away. *Lord, be with her family. Help them find comfort in You.*

Another hour passed as she fed the cow antibiotics to control secondary bacterial infection. It was a waiting game now.

"We've done all we can. We'll have to hope for the best."

"And pray for the good Lord to intervene," Dad added.

"Amen."

He glanced at her, his expression softening. "How are you doing, Jessie?"

Her eyes smarted. He didn't call her Jessie very often these days. He used to, praising her skills with guns and riding when she was small. But then life had gotten busier as she'd turned into a student, desperate to get the high grades to prove she deserved to be one of the lucky few accepted into veterinary school. Their bond had thinned as she'd spent more time at her desk than by his side, and he'd taken Cassie's interest in the ranch as his due. To have uninterrupted time with him like this was special, to be the sole daughter by his side was rare. To have his attention on her felt like gold.

"I'm doing better," she admitted.

"Does doing this," he gestured to the barn, "make you want to return to the veterinary world?"

The lightness of the morning dissipated, like mist after the sun rose and burned. "I still want to help animals. I just can't manage the fast pace like before."

"Have you quit yet?'

"I've got my resignation letter written." Cassie and Hannah had helped write that. Hannah was an expert, having undergone workplace challenges that had seen her switch jobs. Hannah's mom was experienced in women's legal rights, so she knew a thing or two about how to address issues clearly and firmly.

"Any plans to send it?" Dad asked.

"Soon." Once the medical leave of absence ran out. "But quitting means I'll need to find another job, and I don't have it in me to chase that just yet."

"You could always work here."

"I think Cassie would have my hide." Her sister loved the ranch with a passion that ran far deeper than her or Poppy. "Besides, I'd need a paying gig."

"Not if you're staying here too. You know your mom would love to have you stay."

"I'm such a drawcard, that's true." She rolled her eyes.

"We love you," he said gruffly. "Always happy to have you around."

Tears smarted, forcing her to drag in a deep breath. "Love you too."

Silence passed, broken only by the nickering of their horses, as if they carried on a special conversation in the language of whinnying and neighs.

"And I appreciate the suggestion," she eventually said, "but I don't think that Cassie would appreciate me stepping onto her turf."

"Mmm, I'm not sure how much longer she'll want to stay. She's been a little distracted lately with her beau."

"Do you think he'll pop the question soon?" She'd asked Mom the same. It felt like a weird question to ask her father. He wasn't a romantic, even if he did possess a soft heart.

"Don't know. That's their business, I guess."

"But it might affect us—will affect us—if Cassie has to move away."

"I can't rightly see either of them wanting to move from Three Creeks. The man travels so much for work but still needs a place to call home."

And seeing Harrison had next to no family, and had basically been adopted into the James family, the ranch was like his new home base.

She wondered if all men would be so understanding of the strong ties that connected some families. Tom had a close relationship with his folks, too. Cassie had mentioned that after the family showcase.

Miranda strolled past, her chin up and tail aloft like she was on a beauty parade.

"Just as well that cat earns her keep," her dad muttered. She'd brought in another three mice this morning, laying them down like trophies for Jess. It reminded her of when Buster used to do the same.

Buster. A pang hit her. She was lonely without her little companion. It'd be good to have someone to talk to, someone to cuddle, someone to hold at night. And if she couldn't have a certain hockey player with dark curly hair and green eyes, then another animal might be nice.

"Do... do you think it's too soon to get another dog?"

Her father faced her. "Depends on what your plans are. If you're thinking of staying on the ranch, then we have the working dogs, and probably don't need another one. But if you're asking about you, then you need to consider if you're up to looking after one." His mouth twisted wryly. "Of course, I don't need to tell the vet how to suck eggs."

"You gotta take the lid off first." Their old joke.

"Buster was old, but a faithful companion. I think it'd do you good to have a companion to force you out of yourself."

She nodded, as her heart flickered, hungry for the companionship or a dog again. "I'll think about it."

"Pray on it some, too," Dad advised. "Just like we're all praying that God will direct your paths."

"Thanks, Dad."

Her paths. Her future. So much remained unknown. But if she was leaving it in God's capable hands, then she didn't need to fear about what the future might bring. God could be trusted with it all.

Another memory flickered, something else Tom had said. That God held her in the palm of His hands.

Lord, help me to leave my future with You.

She swallowed. *And Tom.*

Thirteen

Their preseason games saw wins at home and in Edmonton. It was nice to play against Ryan Guillemette and see Sylvie, his wife, again. Then they travelled to play Luc in Winnipeg, where he briefly saw Luc's dance partner but now partner-in-life Bailey. Then Vancouver, where he caught up with Zac and Ainsley, and Chris Thomas and his family. Everywhere Tom went it seemed he bumped up against happy couples, expanding families, his friends moving on in their lives while he was left behind puttering along in first gear. Praying daily for patience. Praying daily for wisdom. Asking God to help him to find contentment in the ordinary things.

He was thankful for Benji, thankful for a companion who was happy to run with him, even though the days were getting much colder.

They'd had the first snow of the year, and as Canadian Thanksgiving approached in mid-October, he wondered if it was possible to go see his family. But given their schedule only allowed one day off he didn't think so.

Which left him wondering what to do. In the past Mike and Bree had often held a Thanksgiving spread for teammates who didn't have family near, but they weren't doing that this year. And while he was tempted to spend the day at home, relaxing with Benji, watching Netflix, it also seemed a little lame. Thanksgiving was supposed to be a time to gather with others, to count blessings and savor them. Not just pass in another day of rest.

He listened to the conversations in the locker room, wishing his folks weren't going to Travis's parents' with Michelle and Sadie. Spending all that time travelling to visit someone else's house he didn't know too well didn't sit too right with him.

"What are you doing, Tom?" Mike asked.

"Haven't decided yet."

Franklin glanced at him. "You're not seeing your folks?"

"They're going to my sister's in-laws this year. It's too far, so I didn't want to go."

Franklin nodded, and the way he hesitated made Tom wonder if he was looking to ask Tom to join the James family. But then he didn't, the conversation moved on, and he was struck with a sense of disappointment.

He'd still barely heard from Jess. Barely heard, because she had finally sent him a smiling emoji after his last joke. Which felt like years ago now. And an emoji response was hardly the invitation to open up a new conversation.

But at least if she'd sent that she hadn't blocked him completely from her life. And it might mean she was feeling a little better.

He drove home, microwaved an instant meal recommended by his trainer, and ate in front of the TV as he did most nights. Watching crap on TV was better than letting himself feel the swoop of loneliness, even if Benji snuffled through half his meal in ten seconds flat.

He rubbed his head. "Greedy guts."

Benji lifted his head and eyed him, then resumed eating his kibble. He always took a lot longer to eat the dry dog food, like disappointment made him reluctant as it wasn't all fresh meat.

He stroked him again. The upcoming schedule would see a ten day road trip which he'd reluctantly booked Benji in to a boarding kennel. He was still hoping for an alternative, but it seemed nothing was in his radar. Apart from one option that seemed hopelessly impossible. She'd need to send more than one emoji for him to feel like he could ask that.

His phone buzzed with a text. Franklin.

> Hey, not sure if you have plans for Thanksgiving yet, but you're welcome to join us.

Wow. That made a turnaround. Time with Franklin, Hannah, and probably Hannah's mom would be better than time on his own. He wasn't about to turn a gift-horse down.

> Sure. Want me to bring anything?

> Nope.

His phone buzzed with a call and he answered his mom. She opened by checking he had arrangements for Thanksgiving—feeling bad about his not going to Regina, no doubt—but then it soon became apparent about the real purpose of her phone call.

"So, how are things going with Jess?"

"They're not." He explained how she was taking time off work, needed time to process and heal. "Keep praying for her, Mom."

"And I'll keep praying for you, too. That's not an easy situation to be in."

No sirree.

He ignored a call from Michelle—he knew Mom would pass on whatever he told her, anyway, so there was no point—then went for a run and played with Benji, then got a message from Franklin.

> Change of plan. Having Thanksgiving at Mom and Dad's instead.

Disappointment crawled through his chest. He wished—nope. Not gonna push.

Have fun.

? You're invited too.

He was? Anticipation flared within, lighting every pore. Talk about an answered prayer. "Hallelujah."

Benji barked, as if sensing his excitement. Which sparked an idea.

Can Benji come too?

Of course. One o'clock, lunch. See you then.

He fist-pumped again.

At one on the dot he drove down the long drive to the Three Creek farmhouse. Benji's ears pricked, as if he could tell something exciting was coming his way. He patted the lab. "Almost there, then you can see her again."

He shook his head at himself, knowing his words were as much for himself as for Benji. But the past five weeks had felt much too long. How was she doing? Why hadn't she responded to his messages lately, apart from that one emoji? Was this actually the right thing to do?

He winced, realizing he actually hadn't prayed about it. "Hey God, if You don't want me here, I'll go. Just send me a phone call or make it really plain. I don't want to be a distraction or get in the way."

Nothing but peace filled the interior of the car, so he guessed that was God's okay.

The farmhouse pulled into view, the last of yellow poplars holding onto their leaves in a grim fight against the approach of winter. He parked, noting the other cars, most of which he recognized from previous visits. "Here goes nothing then."

Would she hug him? Want to talk with him? Did she even know he was coming? He hoped his attendance would be a welcome addition.

He exited, then freed Benji from his crate, and he instantly sped off after a rabbit.

"Benji!"

He whistled but for once the dog didn't obey. Clapped his hands, but Benji ignored him still. Excellent. Nothing like arriving for Thanksgiving and losing his dog within the first minute. Sweat slicked his back. Were they super punctual here? Leonie struck him as pretty laidback, but some holidays made people morph into time-management monsters that made life unfun, his sister being one of them.

"Benji!" He whistled again, but still the stubborn dog kept running. "Silly mutt."

"Looks like someone needs dog training lessons."

He froze, his heart thudding. Then, biting back a smile, turned to see her on the porch, leaning against a post. "Do you know anyone who can help with that?"

Jess smiled, and he caught a glimpse of who she had been before. Not the shadow of herself from his last visit. Not the stressed woman he'd seen earlier this year. But the one at last year's wedding, who had danced with him like she didn't have a care in the world. Who had held him captive with her smile and blue-green eyes and had never let him go.

He swallowed. "Hi."

"Hi." Her voice was soft.

"You're looking better." Less pale, less thin, less shadowed.

"Thanks. I'm feeling a little better."

He took a step closer, then paused. He hungered to know what had helped—had he?—but wouldn't push. "It's good to see you."

Her cheeks pinked, and she ducked her head, her attention

soon veering to Benji, still doing zoomies as if thrilled to be set free on a ranch again.

Of course. His heart dipped. He should've expected her to prefer to focus on Benji to him. What was he doing fooling himself into thinking she'd like to see him? She'd only sent an emoji. He sighed.

"What is it?"

He didn't want to say he was jealous of a dog. But the spike in his heart when Benji noticed her, and instantly changed course and headed her direction said he was.

But he couldn't be too jealous, not when he heard her laughter, nor saw the way she wrapped Benji in a big hug. "I missed you."

Judging from the way Benji was doing his best to lick her face, "He missed you too."

She leaned back, peering up at him, her gaze catching his. "I missed him as well."

His heart stuttered. Did she mean to imply that her earlier comment meant she had missed him?

But before he could test that, Franklin joined them at the front door. "You made it. Come on, Mom's dishing up."

"Uh, okay." Tom glanced at Jess. "I hope it's okay that we're here."

"I'm glad you are."

Pleasure bloomed across his chest.

He followed her down the hall, washed up, then joined the others at the dining table. Everyone except Poppy, back in Winnipeg, was here, including Harrison, and Hannah's mom.

Tom greeted them all then turned to Leonie. "Thank you for having me here. It means a lot."

"We're glad you could make it."

Derek said the same. "Good to see you again, Son."

He took the seat next to Jess and Benji instantly positioned himself between them. "Uh, is it okay if Benji is inside? He's usually very good, although he will guilt anyone who looks at him into giving him treats. Which is fine, as long as it's in small portions."

"We're more used to outside dogs, but he can stay seeing he's so well-behaved."

"Apart from when he was chasing that rabbit before," he muttered.

"He must like it here," Cassie said.

"There's a lot to like," Harrison said, giving her a squeeze around the shoulders.

That was for sure. Good food, good company, and the smile of the woman sitting next to him. Which she was aiming at him now.

"What kind of dog chases anything red?" Jess asked.

She was making a joke? Everyone else seemed to be holding their breath, too. "What kind?" he asked.

"A bulldog."

He laughed. "What did the skeleton say to the puppy?"

She smiled. "What?"

"Bon appetit."

That drew more laughter, and even Derek cracked a smile. "It must be time to say grace."

They joined hands, and Tom tried to concentrate on the prayer and not the feel of Jess's hand in his.

Tempted as he was to keep the nerves at bay by cracking a few more one-liners, he did his best to stay focused. But having Jess seated beside him felt like such a miracle compared to what he'd felt lately.

Conversation swirled around. Cassie and Harrison shared about *As The Heart Draws*, which was due to finish filming soon, before a scheduled zombie movie in October.

"A zombie movie?" Tom asked Cassie, who oversaw these things. That didn't exactly fit the down-to-earth wholesome family vibes of the James ranch.

"Are you sure you want to do that?" Franklin asked his sister.

"It pays the bills. And it's low budget—"

"Imagine that," Franklin muttered.

"Hey, I've seen the script," Cassie sounded offended. "There's nothing weird in it."

"Apart from zombies."

Tom peeked at Jess who had her own lips pressed together. The siblings' argument didn't include her. "Why do zombies never eat comedians?" he murmured.

Her mouth curved. "Why?"

"They taste funny."

She laughed, and he felt like doing another fist pump of celebration.

Cassie arched her brows. "Care to share?"

"Sorry. Just a dumb joke."

Derek nodded to Tom. "I appreciate you making Jessie smile."

He nodded, cheeks heating, and scooped in another mouthful of mashed potatoes.

Benji stirred, and he patted him. He'd seen the way Benji had scooted under the table, and suspected Jess wasn't the only one offering him little tid-bits of food.

Conversation shifted to the upcoming season's game schedule, and he shared about the upcoming away games.

"What will you do with Benji?" Leonie asked.

He winced. "I had to book him into a boarding kennel."

Jess's eyes widened. "You're going to stick him in a kennel?"

"It's not ideal, but I don't have anyone else to ask."

"You could ask me."

The world seemed to shrink down to just them. "You'd look after him?"

She patted Benji. "He's a gorgeous dog. And I'd like to." She glanced back at her folks. "If Mom and Dad agree."

Did that mean she planned to stay on the ranch?

Cassie seemed to think the same as she asked Jess that same question.

"I don't know yet what I want to do," Jess admitted quietly.

"But I don't want to work in that same type of environment. It's not healthy for me."

Not healthy for anyone, if her friend's situation had been challenged by it too.

"Hey, I'd love for you to look after Benji. It'd only be part-time," he assured. "I could come get him the rest of the time."

"I think you might find he'd want to stay," Leonie said, a twinkle in her eye.

"That's right." Cassie grinned. "Ranch life is a good life."

"He'd certainly have a lot more to explore here than in my tiny backyard," he admitted. And if Benji did stay on a more permanent basis, then maybe Tom would have more of a reason to come visit regularly. But he'd miss the furry goofball. Which reminded him. "I actually should talk to my sister, seeing Benji was hers originally."

"Of course you should," Jess said.

He smiled at her, appreciating her understanding. It might be early days yet, but she seemed so much better, the light in her eyes like what he remembered from before, her features suffused with something that looked like peace.

Leonie nodded. "Now, who is ready for homemade apple pie?"

"Yes, please," rang the chorus around the table.

But the promise of pie, sweet as it was, was nothing compared to this feeling of gladness that Jess seemed so much better. And that maybe things with Jess might finally tip into something more than this awkward stop-start friendship, and have time to one day develop into something real.

JESS HUGGED BENJI CLOSE, wondering how many times Tom had done just the same. Was that a trace of his aftershave on the dog's coat? She inhaled deeply, knowing that made her weird, but she didn't care. This past year meant she'd felt plenty weird, and had little shame left to lose.

"Do you miss him like I do?" she whispered.

Benji woofed, then turned and licked her cheek.

She chuckled. "I'll take that as a yes."

Tom's question to his sister about Benji staying on the ranch while he was away had met with an instant yes. And his road trip following Thanksgiving had drawn the excuse that Jess could message him regularly, just to let him know how Benji was getting on, of course.

She'd talked it over with God, and sensed a yes, it was okay to get back into the pattern of regular communication with Tom again. Especially because she was starting her day with Bible reading and prayer, doing her best to stay in the rhythms of grace with God, sensing His presence daily.

She needed to do so, because one smile from Tom at Thanksgiving had been enough to plummet her from the precipice of ignoring Tom into the land of extreme liking. He'd always possessed a warm affability, and it was that quality, that ease of his that meant he got on so well with her family, that had helped her relax again.

Thanksgiving meals were always amazing, but it was the board games afterward that had been more fun. Playing Pictionary as Tom's partner, trying to decipher his scrawl, had provoked more laughter than she remembered all year.

Then his dumb jokes, including plenty about Thanksgiving.

"What side of a turkey has more feathers? The outside."

"If you call a large turkey a gobbler, what do you call a small one? A goblet."

"What's a turkey's favorite Thanksgiving food? Nothing, it's already stuffed."

Cassie had laughed and given the thumbs up. Harrison and Dad got on with him well, too. Even Hannah's mom had asked Jess quietly how long they had been dating, to which she'd had to admit they weren't, even though the words had triggered something deep within.

She did want to date Tom. She knew that now. But there remained so many unknowns still, not least about what to do about her work.

Hannah and Hannah's mom had given her the courage to finally press send on her resignation email, after which she'd blocked her Mail on her computer so she wouldn't have to see Dr. Theo's angry response. He'd invested a lot of time in her, and she was one hundred percent certain he'd think his time spent on her was wasted.

But she couldn't look at the past. She had to let go and look to the future. To what God had for her. "Which is what?" she whispered, chin dipped on Benji's head.

Benji squirmed, like he didn't want her to hold him like this.

She relaxed her hold a little. What to do, what to do…

"Lord, what do you want me to do?"

She closed her eyes, heart easing a little. She might like helping her dad around the ranch and feeling useful that way, but there was something about holding Benji, remembering how much she enjoyed smaller animals like this that helped her feel ease.

"Lord, is there a way I could work with dogs and cats? Maybe at another vet clinic when I'm feeling stronger? If there is, could You please show me a way?"

Benji licked her again, and she hugged him near. Then wished that instead of the dog, she could hug his owner instead.

FOURTEEN

The puck sped across the ice, and Tom one-timed it to the Seattle net. Goal!

The red light lit and his Lenny Kravitz goal song blared as his teammates thumped his back. "Great goal, man," Franklin said.

"Can't make a goal like that without a pass like yours." He skated to fist-bump his teammates and took his seat as his line was replaced by the next. He grabbed a drink, a time-out stopping play, allowing a moment to look across the ice into the crowd.

She'd come? His pulse skittered. He lifted a hand. Jess waved back. He grinned.

"You see who is here tonight?" Franklin asked.

"I'm glad she made it."

Franklin nodded. "Want to come out with us tonight? Hannah is off tonight"—a rare thing—"but she thought it'd be a good chance to talk with Jess. I think Jess would appreciate you being there, too."

"Sounds good." He didn't want to seem too eager, but hello? That was a one thousand percent *Yes*.

Messaging Jess about Benji was one thing, but it wasn't what he really wanted. He wanted to know how she was doing. For real. But the fact she was looking after his dog while he was away made him feel a little like they were co-parenting. That they were in a relationship of sorts, even if it was just minding a dog.

It gave him the excuse to go out to the ranch before he had to travel for a game, or she'd come to his condo. They'd swap dog anecdotes, then keep on talking.

All very careful, nothing too personal, even if he got the chance to ask how she was doing. She might say she was fine, and was definitely looking happier than when he'd seen her several months ago, but their conversations were still a little too shallow for him to be truly satisfied.

They beat Seattle—Kyle Tinker's shooting prowess was no match for Franklin and Mike's rock solid defense, a number one defense pairing that was touted as one of the best across the league. Tom joined the others in lifting his stick and acknowledging their supporters, pointing out those fans that held placards like they thought this was the playoffs.

He skated closer to the family and friends section, and somehow through the crowd caught Jess's eyes. She smiled, mouthed "good job."

Her affirmation ballooned warmth through his chest. The fact she'd seen him play, and play well—yes, he might've showed off a little for her—meant so much.

He wanted her to see him as more than just the owner of a dog that she spent time with. He wanted her to see him as more than just a friend. But they'd never get beyond this seesaw of tiptoed distanced friendship unless she finally opened up and shared. Which meant maybe he'd finally have to screw up enough courage to ask the questions he hadn't yet. Questions that might just get an answer tonight.

FRANKLIN AND HANNAH'S apartment was fairly utilitarian, which suited a busy couple whose work took them away frequently.

"Come in, come in."

He moved to hug Hannah, but she leaned back. "Sorry. I've been feeling a little sick lately, and I don't want you to catch whatever it is I've got."

"I'm sorry to hear that. I don't have to stay if you'd prefer."

"No, that's fine. And I get the feeling if we don't do this now then it might not happen. Carpe diem, seize the day, and all that kind of thing."

"Sure." He was happy to jump on board the seize-the-moment train. Seizing the moment with Jess was his modus operandi, even if she still remained a little aloof with him.

"So, what's this all about?"

Hannah glanced at Franklin who nodded. Then she began. "Okay, so I was chatting with some of the guys who do the social media for the team, and they just so happened to mention about an upcoming post where the players do their 'see who has the fastest dog on ice' thing." She smiled at Tom. "I wondered if you'd been approached about including Benji."

"Uh, I might've seen an email but I can't remember too many details."

"Could you find that email? I think you should enter Benji."

"Why?"

"Because it could be really good for your profile. You know, give that warm and fuzzy feeling when people think about you. It makes you more than a one dimensional hockey player in people's minds."

"Okay..." But he knew what she meant. Some of hockey's tough guys seemed pretty intentional about letting people know they had a pet. It indicated a softer side, and seemed a way in for people to support them, buy their jerseys, invest in the team. And while he wasn't known as a tough guy by any means, it never hurt to show the team he was a player that the fans loved. Someone who was worth keeping around and re-signing when his current contract expired. Getting rid of a fan favorite was never a good look for a team.

"I thought you mentioned this has something to do with me," Jess said.

"Well, yes." Hannah glanced between them. "Seeing you both share Benji's care I thought you might like to know."

"But he's Tom's dog."

"Yes." Hannah glanced at Franklin who finally spoke.

"So, what Hannah didn't mention, is that this could also be an opportunity for you."

"How?"

"If you are known as a vet who deals with high profile athletes' dogs, then maybe you could find some work that way."

"But how would I do that?" She shook her head. "I've gone to a game, Franklin, but it doesn't mean I'm ready to be more upfront than that. What if Dr. Theo sees me?"

"You don't need to worry about him," Hannah said. "You've resigned, and you owe him nothing. From that discussion with my mom and lawyer it seems he might owe you compensation, but I can understand you might not want to pursue that."

"Compensation?" Tom asked, studying Jess.

She grimaced. "Hannah's mom thinks I might be entitled to something for the amount of overtime I did, especially with the dog training that I never really saw extra pay for. But I don't care about the money. It wouldn't be that much anyway, so I don't think it's worth the hassle."

"It's not about the amount but the principle," Hannah said. "Look, I fully respect your decision if you decide not to pursue things, but it doesn't change the fact that you still need to consider what to do about the future."

"When Hannah first mentioned the idea to me I thought it seemed like a really good way to get involved back in the veterinary industry again," Franklin said. "You could get a few clients, ones who could pay and who *would* pay, because they have a public profile to protect."

She shuddered. "As long as none of them dye their dogs pink."

Tom smiled. "I doubt any hockey player is foolish enough to allow that."

"It's not the hockey players I'm concerned with as much as their influencer other halves."

Ah. Like that Giselle character from months ago.

"I think it's a good idea," Tom said. "You might not need to work every day but could pick the hours that suit you. And you could determine who you see, who your clients are—and aren't. None of us want you to feel like you have to deal with people who are mean."

"That makes me sound so weak," she murmured.

"Not weak," Tom corrected, "but wise. You don't need to place yourself in a situation where people are going to undermine you or make you feel uncomfortable in any way. And look, if it helps at all, I'm really happy to be the first to sign up for the Dr. Jessie James clinic."

"Fastest vet in the west," Franklin quipped.

She shook her head. "I wouldn't want that to be my motto. That was part of the problem, having to see clients so quickly and make a decision, then move on to the next one. How can a vet make the correct decision if they're rushed all the time?"

"We can come up with a better motto," Hannah promised. "But... do you think it's a good idea?"

Jess bit her lip, and he prayed for her, hoping she'd say yes.

She turned to him. "What do you think, Tom?"

"I think you shouldn't let all those years of training go to waste," he said gently. "I think this is a good opportunity."

"But wouldn't all those hockey players already have vets in place?"

"Most would, yes," Hannah admitted. "But people change vets all the time, so there's nothing stopping you from promoting yourself as someone they should one day change to."

"I think Mike would be happy to switch to you," Franklin said.

"That's two," Tom encouraged.

Jess smiled. "I don't know if it counts when I'm looking after Benji half the time anyway."

"It totally counts," he assured.

They tossed ideas back and forth, until eventually she nodded. "Okay. I agree it's a good idea. I'll look into it."

Hannah smiled and sat back in her seat. "We should get you a website, which means you'd need a name for your practice. Maybe Poppy can help—she's done that before, hasn't she? And I could find out if the race has a sponsor. If not, maybe you could sponsor the race. Or be the vet who runs the race."

"They probably have someone already," Franklin said.

"Possibly, but it never hurts to see if they have a contract for next year."

Tom studied Jess, who seemed overwhelmed by all the questions and decisions to be made. "But Jess." He leaned forward, sorely tempted to hold her hand. Not that he would while Franklin watched him. "You don't have to make any decisions right now. Think about it, take some time, you don't need to rush. It's your decision to make, but weigh out the pros and cons. Because while it is a good idea, there will no doubt be some costs associated with it."

She nodded. "It costs a lot to set up your own practice."

"But if you only have a few clients, and you schedule home visits, then it's not like you need a dedicated clinic space."

Her demeanor brightened. "I hadn't thought of that."

"You could refer more challenging patients to other hospitals, people that you know you can trust."

She nodded. "I know that Dr. Theo wanted me to do some visits for some of the more wealthy clients who wanted to stay private, but I hadn't thought about it in this context."

"Maybe you should. It could be a good opportunity for you."

She nodded slowly. "It could be."

And he prayed she'd be encouraged, not overwhelmed.

Setting up her own clinic? It seemed like a crazy dream. Impossible. But something in Hannah's words had ignited within, lighting a fire of a long ago dream where she'd imagined exactly that. And then there had been something about the way Tom had encouraged her, his wise words steadying her, helping her step back from falling into a sense of overwhelm, and reminding her it might sound huge, but it was possible, even doable. If she wanted.

She exhaled, her hand clasping Tom's arm as together they walked down the stairs at Franklin's apartment. "Thank you for saying what you said before."

"I said a lot of things. Which one?"

"About not needing to make a decision right now. I have to admit it felt a little overwhelming."

He paused, and her feet slowed too. "You need to feel like you can do this. Not just get swept up in an idea then feel like you're being dragged out to sea by somebody's else's enthusiasm. It needs to be a decision you own. Not anybody else's."

She nodded. He was wise this man.

"What's that look for?" he asked. "Did I say something wrong?"

"No. Just the opposite. You keep surprising me by saying all the right things."

"Wow. Rude." His mouth's half-curve said that was tease.

Still she felt the need to assure him. She didn't want him mad at her. "I didn't mean it like that. I really do value your opinion."

The tease faded from his features as a more serious, intent expression took its place. "I care about you, Jess. You know that."

She nodded. She did. She lowered her gaze, suddenly unable to look at him, unable to cope with his kindness. For goodness sake. If she couldn't cope with this man who said he cared for her, how on earth was she going to cope with dealing with clients again, many of whom wouldn't think twice about how they spoke to her when caught in the middle of worry about their pet?

"Is my t-shirt really so fascinating?"

Her gaze jerked back to his face, and she realized she'd been staring at his chest. His very nice chest, as she recalled from the river so many weeks ago. Had it been over two months already?

"I'm sorry."

"Hey." He lifted a hand as if to touch her then dropped it, leaving her with a feeling of disconcerting loss.

"You don't need to apologize." His lips curved higher. "I'm kind of flattered that you'd want to check out my impressive muscles."

Laughter barked from her, bouncing around the stairwell.

"What? I didn't think it was that funny."

She shoved him, but her hand sizzled at the touch of his skin.

He seemed to feel it too, staring at her, all humor drained away, replaced by an intensity she'd never seen before.

"What is it?" she whispered.

He blinked, then shook his head. "We should go. It's getting late."

She nodded, and let him walk her to her car. He stayed as she got in and wound down the window. The perfect gentleman.

"When are you next going away?" she asked, as if she didn't already know. She had his schedule burned in her brain, and knew exactly which days she might see him.

"On Saturday."

She nodded. "So, when do you want me to come and collect Benji? Saturday morning? Friday night?"

She tensed. Did saying that when he was looking at her like that make him think she was hinting for a date? Which she wasn't. Well, not really. But if he was to offer, then she might not turn him down.

He blew out a breath. Placed a hand on the top of the car. "It might be best if I drop him at the ranch on Friday night. If you think your parents are okay with that."

"Of course they are." Her parents liked Benji, and Mom loved Tom as another son. Dad was a fan, too. Maybe it was the fact that Tom was always kind, and even though he might know way too many bad dad jokes, it showed his cheerful spirit which made for a mood-lifter wherever he went. He was a blessing to be around, she realized. Never negative, always upbeat. A good guy.

"Okay. Would... would you be wanting to stay for dinner?"

Offering him dinner was the chance to test the waters, so to speak. Was he interested in her, or was he simply wanting her for her superior dog-minding skills?

He scratched his chin, studying her, as if this was a million dollar question. "If you think they'd be okay with that," he murmured, "then that would be great."

She smiled, and his serious expression faded, replaced by a smile of his own. "It's a date, then."

"A date, then." He nodded, and that look of intensity returned.

FIFTEEN

Having dinner with a woman, her parents and sister, and a dog, definitely did *not* factor into any dates he'd imagined with Jess. But seeing this was all he could get for right now, he'd make the most of it.

Judging from the way she hadn't looked at him much, had barely touched him let alone given him one of those huge hugs that he still relived in his dreams, he wondered if she was feeling the strain of being on show in front of her family. But while there were some tiny lines around her eyes he didn't recall seeing last year, she didn't seem to wear other signs of constraint. Which made him wonder if her talk of dates was just something he'd misread, and gotten too excited about, when clearly she was not in a space to be romantic.

See? This was not a date. *Not* a date, he told himself firmly. Just a chance to eat, drop Benji off for a few days, then pick him up on Wednesday.

"So, how do you feel about playing Vancouver and Seattle?" Derek asked.

"Vancouver will be tougher, for sure." Zac Parotti was the NHL's leading goal scorer. Again. "Kyle Tinker is good, but Parotti is better."

Cassie asked her mom a question about Christmas, which made him wonder if he'd earn another invitation. They had more days off for Christmas, which meant he probably should go see his folks, even if he'd rather be here, playing Dad to a dog who appeared to love his adopted Mom a little bit more. Maybe that had something to do with the treats she kept sneaking him.

He leaned a little closer. "Is there a reason you keep feeding my dog bits from your plate?"

"Um, I think you'll find that when he's here he's my dog."

"Is that so?"

"Extremely so."

Her gaze, direct and clear, held a challenge and a smirk. He loved it.

"Fine. But if I have to take him to the doc I hope you know you'll be paying."

"Fine."

"Good."

His veins pulsed with a new kind of energy. This banter was different for them, energizing for him, and it seemed for her too. Her eyes held a sparkle he hadn't seen for a long time.

He leaned a little closer. "I hope you know a good one."

"A good one what?" she murmured.

"A good veterinarian."

"Mm, I might." She eyed him. "It depends on what you think counts as good."

"Someone who knows her stuff, who tells it straight, who doesn't charge a bomb but isn't giving her services away for free because she knows her worth."

She studied him.

"What are you two discussing?" Cassie asked. Now *As The Heart Draws* had wrapped, Harrison was off filming a TV episode of Lincoln Cash's police detective show in Toronto. "Just in case," he'd said.

As in, just in case *As The Heart Draws* was not renewed after this season. They had to cast a new lead actress, seeing as Ainsley

Beckett—Zac Parotti's fiancée—had stepped away. Zac had said in a Bible study chat group that she would return for occasional episodes, but it'd be more like a cameo for that particular school-marm cowgirl to fulfil contractual obligations, rather than anything major like what she did now, where her character basically anchored each episode.

"We're discussing how Jess should not undervalue herself when she starts doing her freelance veterinary consultations," he finally answered.

"I think this is a great idea of Hannah's," Leonie said. "I would hate to think of all your hard work going to waste. You are such a talent, Jess. You should stay involved."

She nodded. "I will."

He fist-pumped internally. "Good."

"So, tell us how this will work. What do you need to do to set up your own business? Do you need to buy equipment? Get registered in some way?" Cassie asked.

Jess tensed, her hands clenching in her lap. So many questions. Too many questions. "I don't know," she admitted. It was enough she was considering doing it, rather than getting stressed by all the unknowns.

He placed a hand on Benji's head, as he rested between them. "What do you think is a great vet care name? Apart from Jessie James, that is."

Jess rolled her eyes, her shoulders dropping a little as she relaxed.

"What about Dr. Spot?"

"That sounds like someone from *Star Trek*." Cassie wrinkled her nose. "I'm not feeling it."

"Yeah, that was bad. How about Paws in Boots?"

Leonie chuckled. "That sounds like a clinic for dogs with broken legs."

"What about Purr-gent Care?"

"I like J. James Veterinary Practice," Jess stated.

He nodded. "Simple, straightforward, but effective. I like it."

"It's what I always imagined I'd call my vet clinic if I was lucky enough to run one someday."

"And here you are. At some day." He grinned. "Living your dream."

Her lips lifted, her gaze soft yet more sure, and again he felt that sense of victory.

He'd do anything to see that sapphire-glint in her eye, to see her relaxed, feeling confident enough to own her choices, own her future, rather than feel trapped by the decisions of others.

A glance across the table saw Derek meet his eye and slowly nod, like he was giving his blessing for something that Tom wasn't even sure was ready to happen yet. This wasn't a date. This was family time. But it felt like a step closer to the future he wanted. One where Jess trusted him enough to share her heart, and rather than share a dog, they shared a last name and a home.

He blinked. Exhaled. Studied his own nervous fingers. He sure hoped Derek and Leonie hadn't read that in his face. It was way too soon for thoughts like that.

Benji whined, moving to rest his head on Jess's thigh, his eyes focused on her as if willing her to give him more food.

Tom stifled a snicker.

"What's going on over there?" Cassie asked.

"Nothing. Just the usual. Benji thinks Jess is a soft touch and is pleading with his big brown eyes for her to give him more food."

"That's because he knows she is a soft touch."

"I can't help it. He's very sweet, aren't you, boy?" Jess rubbed Benji's ears.

"He loves you."

Benji's head tilted, his dark eyes reflecting Tom's face, as the words rebounded to hit him in the heart.

Benji might love Jessie, but Tom loved her more. He *loved* her. Loved her kindness, loved her passion, loved her faith and clear-headed direction. She made him want to be a better man, to push himself to be worthy of her. And while she might've friend-zoned him at the moment, he couldn't help but trust that God might soften her heart and help her see him as someone she might want in her future. His heart thumped. In *their* future.

He grasped his water, slugged it down in one gulp.

"You okay there, Son?" Derek asked.

"Yep."

A grandfather clock chimed eight beats, which seemed to prompt Derek's yawns. Eight might not be late for some, but it seemed it was for this rancher.

Tom glanced at his watch. Yep. He should go.

"I have an early flight and need to get going. But thank you for a lovely meal."

"It's always a pleasure having you come," Leonie said. "You can come any time."

"Thanks."

He kissed Leonie's cheek, shook Derek's hand, gave Cassie a quick hug, then turned to Jess. "Walk me out?"

She nodded, and they departed, Benji trotting between them. He rubbed his dog's head, then turned to Jess. "Thanks again for looking after him."

"Any time."

He nodded. Wondered how to prolong this time snatched with her, even though it was cold.

Then she shivered.

"You should go in. I'll see you Wednesday."

"I'll see you Sunday," she said.

"You're coming to the game?" he asked quickly.

"I meant I'll see you on TV," she amended.

His heart settled back into normal. See? Way too soon to think she wanted to see him specifically. "Okay, well, take care of yourself."

"You too. Don't get too banged up."

"I don't plan to."

For some reason, his hand propelled out, like he was about to give her a handshake. But kissing her cheek felt too intimate, and hugging her felt even more so. The distance she seemed to like was best served by a handshake.

She looked down at his outstretched hand then half shrugged and clasped it. Palm to palm, his fingers wrapping around hers.

Then suddenly he felt the urge to get closer, so drew her nearer so she tilted in, and as their hands still clasped between them, gave her a little one-armed hug as he gently kissed her cheek.

MEN who only wished to remain friends with a woman really shouldn't kiss their cheeks.

Jess hadn't been able to escape the memory of her cheek against Tom's bristly one, not the way her senses had ignited as if fireworks had been ignited. He smelled three million times better than fireworks though, something sweet yet spicy that seemed to tantalize her nerve endings. Then he'd pulled back, all too quick, the imprint of his lips on her skin indelible.

Oh, she wished she was braver, had been brave enough to turn her cheek and meet his lips with hers. Yet that time was not yet. *Not yet*, she marveled at herself. It would be one day, though. She knew that beyond a doubt. The two of them shared more than a dog, they shared a bond.

And February 14 might be over three months away, but she felt she'd definitely found a Valentine for a vet.

As promised, she and Benji watched his game against Vancouver, cheering on Franklin as he scored a goal. And she might've commented a few too many times on Tom's assist, seeing the way her family eyed her, like they couldn't understand why she was more excited about that than Franklin's rare goal.

But watching Tom play, she was getting new insight into this man. He was generous—he probably could've scored himself, but instead he gave the scoring chance to his teammate. Even though Zac Parotti was on the opposite team Tom was friendly, making a rare smile cross Zac's face. Probably another of his dumb jokes.

"I like him," Cassie said.

"Who, Zac?"

Cassie threw a piece of popcorn at her. "Don't play dumb. You know who I mean."

"I like him, too," Mom said.

"I have to admit I wasn't a fan of his joking around all the time, but he's growing on me," Dad said.

"I think the fact he makes Jess laugh is a win."

"Mom's right. You need someone who can make you smile," Cassie said to Jess. "You can be too intense."

"But he's more than someone who makes her smile," Mom said. "He's very thoughtful, too."

Cassie smiled. "Sounds like you've got everyone's blessing."

"Blessing for what?" she asked, not daring to say out loud what she'd hoped.

"Oh my goodness, Jess," Cassie exclaimed. "Stop acting dumb. You know we hate it when you do. It doesn't suit you at all."

She shrugged. "There's nothing to bless, anyway." He'd kissed her cheek, not her lips. She shivered. "Besides, I don't know what Poppy or Franklin think."

"Poppy is a definite fan."

"How do you know that?"

"We've been talking in the sister chat."

One of those apps she wasn't privy to anymore since deleting a bunch of apps from her phone. "And Franklin?"

"Come on. He's Tom's teammate. If Franklin doesn't approve it's only because he's got his own issues he's worried about."

That sounded like Cassie knew things that Jess wasn't privy to. "Like?"

Cassie shook her head. "It's not my news to tell."

"News?" Mom sat upright. "Do you mean to say—?"

"Oh, I'm not saying anything."

"Is Hannah—?"

"Don't say it out loud, Mom. If you do, then I can't lie." Cassie turned to Jess. "Don't you say anything either. Oh, man. I can't believe it. I'm going to my room to call Harrison. Good night."

Dad opened a bleary eye. "Why is Cassie storming off?"

"I think she might've accidentally spilled the beans about something that she might not be meant to know."

"About what?" Dad yawned. "I swear, this intermission is going on forever. I think I need to sleep too. Good night." He kissed Mom and smiled at Jess and departed.

Mom looked so pepped up she might never sleep again. But neither of them said anything, just smiling at each other like they were filled with good tidings, in a game of chicken to see who'd spill first.

Jess finally cracked. "I wonder when they might say something?"

"I've heard that twelve weeks can often be a time when people might wish to share important things."

Which could put things at any time. Might they share at Christmas?

"How do you think Cassie knows something when we don't?"

"That is a question for Cassie."

"Oh, wouldn't it be exciting? Franklin would make a great —"

"Don't say it. We don't want to get it wrong. It's their news to share. *If* it's even what we think it is."

"Okay."

But imagining her brother as a dad made her heart squishy. Was this how Tom felt about being an uncle? He loved his little niece, so quite possibly.

She wondered how Hannah felt about it, if it was the case. She'd always been so career focused, that having a baby would definitely mean some adjustments.

But wasn't that how life worked out? There weren't guarantees, and a man might plan his course but God established their paths.

Just like what had happened to her. She might've thought working in a veterinary clinic was once her dream, but this year had taught her that maybe God had ways of nudging people's hearts towards other goals that might align their path more to His best plans for them.

And if working at Dr. Theo's clinic wasn't God's best for her, what was?

She closed her eyes, trying to imagine a future where she had her own clinic, just like she used to when she was young.

But the fragments refused to slip into place like they used to, and instead her heart yearned for other things. Like Benji, whose head rested on her lap. And maybe a baby or two of her own. Like Bree Vaughan, who delighted in motherhood, even if four kids seemed like twice as many as she'd prefer. Jess liked the idea of two kids, one with her own blue eyes, one with green eyes like his—

Her eyes snapped open, her cheeks hot. Thank goodness her mother wasn't like Daniel from the Bible, able to interpret dreams!

The TV showed the game had resumed, the Flames skating on once more. There was Mike, there was Franklin, there—her heart double-thumped—was Tom.

"You know who I think would make a great father?" her mother said dreamily, as if forgetting their silent pact to not speak of it.

"Mom—" she warned.

"Tom."

"Mom!" Did she have some dream interpreting ability after all?

"And no, not just because of his ability to tell dad jokes, like Cassie and Franklin tease him about. He's simply a lovely kind man. The kind of young man I've always wanted for my daughters to marry one day."

She couldn't say anything. Except... "We're not even going out, Mom."

"I know. But a mother can pray, can't she?"

"Isn't it against Mom code to say things like that? What if Tom never asks me?"

"Oh, he will. But he's wise, and patient too. I'm sure he's waiting until you have found your feet again, and can see a future with him. So don't let fears about the unknown get in the way of what might just be God's best."

She swallowed. "Are you saying that you think Tom might be God's best for me?" Her heart fluttered at the prospect.

"Obviously I'm not God, and I don't ascribe to the view that there is only one person in the world who is destined to be your perfect partner. I think that viewpoint really limits God, and we know God is able to do exceedingly above and beyond all we can imagine." Her mom smiled. "When I see Tom I think he'd make a great partner in life for you. Like your father and I. Two people who are different, yet who are molded by God to perfectly complement each other in life."

"This conversation feels like way too much when he hasn't even asked me out," Jess murmured.

"But it doesn't hurt to consider what kind of man makes you happy. And that one," Mom gestured to the screen where the camera was focused on Tom, "brings you joy."

Benji gave a sleepy-sounding woof, like a canine *Amen*.

And she spent the rest of the game watching, wondering, and praying that God would protect Tom.

And that God would direct their paths.

Sixteen

The arena was filled with families, friends and fans, all here for the charity day that included a family favourite which would see the players' dogs race on ice. Tom held Benji's leash, wearing a dog hoodie bearing his jersey number fifteen. Unlike some of the dogs here, Benji didn't seem too fazed by all the color and noise. He'd already posed for photos with Tom on the way in. Been oohed and ahhed at by a dozen people. Tom had him shake hands with a couple of kids who were the team's special guests as part of today's charity for sick kids.

"Okay, are you ready?"

Jess drew in a deep breath and nodded. "I still can't believe I agreed to this."

"Look, it might not be exactly what Hannah suggested, but it's good for you to meet some of the other players. And if we get a chance to talk about your veterinary services to a wider audience, then that's a bonus, right?"

She nodded.

And yes, he wasn't above training Benji to try to win, using the last couple of visits to the ranch to practice Benji running fifty feet to where Jess waited with a treat. Call him sneaky but he'd do all he could to see her get the reward she deserved. And if winning meant people booked her brand new J. James Veterinary Practice, then that made all this worthwhile. The fact that he'd gotten to spend more time with Jess was just a bonus.

He wrapped his arm around her shoulder. "You've got this. And God's got you, okay?"

She glanced up at him, and the noise faded at the sweet look she gave him. "You always know the right thing to say."

"Ditto."

It might be cold in here, but right now he could be on a tropical island with the warmth that swelled within. He loved this woman. He pressed a quick kiss to her cheek, heard her inhalation of breath. "I should let you go get ready."

She nodded, bent to give Benji a quick hug, then joined Bree who was waiting for her. He watched as they gingerly made their way down the ice to the other blue line.

God bless Bree for introducing Jess to a few more of the players' wives and girlfriends. Jess already knew a few players, thanks to being Franklin's sister, but this was a different feel where she wasn't here because of her brother but because of him. Franklin, having no dog, wasn't involved in this part of today's activities at all. So the fact she was here today for Tom's sake, not her brother's, made today feel like they were a couple, even though they hadn't yet had a date. But if things went the way he hoped, then maybe they could finally see a win on that front soon too.

The beagle belonging to Kurt Matthews, the goalie, started yapping, clearly anxious. Mike's Thumper had drawn "awws" from the crowd when he was introduced. The players' pooches ranged from larger dogs like a husky and Tom's Labrador to a French bulldog and a Chihuahua. They were directed to their lanes. The race would be from blue line to blue line, and he would release Benji to run down to Jess at the other end.

"But the others are all wives or girlfriends," she'd murmured. "What am I going to say if I'm asked about that?"

"You won't have to say anything," he'd promised. He'd told today's announcer that Jess was his friend. That was enough for now. Although he'd love for this to become an annual event, and see her have girlfriend status one year, and wife the next. Not that he'd freak anyone out by saying that aloud.

The team's announcer asked them to take their places, then a spotlight shone on each player and pet as they were introduced.

"And in lane three we have the Flames number fifteen, Tom Chavez, and his pet pooch Benji."

A roar came from the crowd as Tom waved. He nudged Benji closer, pointing out where Jess waited, fifty feet away. She was smiling, crouching, her focus on him. A yap from the bulldog next door distracted Benji, so Tom redirected Benji's attention from the bulldog back to Jess, whose smile said she was enjoying this more than she thought.

"Players, are we ready?"

"Come on Benji. Get ready to run to Jess."

"In three, two, one. Go!"

This might just be a dog race, but Tom felt the surge of adrenaline as much as if this had been a game day. "Go to Jess!" he urged, as Benji began his loping run.

Jess stood at the other end, waving her arms to get Benji's attention, and he zeroed in on her. Unlike some of the other pups, who veered off course, or stopped altogether, or sniffed each others' butts. Nope. Benji knew what to do, and was running, running—wait. The French bulldog was in the mix?

"Come on Benji!" he yelled, which was a mistake as Benji hesitated, looking around.

Shoot. "Go to Jess!" he shouted instead.

"Come on Benji!" Jess called, and Benji refocused, once again running to her.

The beagle had paused, Mike's Thumper had trotted back to Mike, who was shaking his head.

The French bulldog had veered to the side where the team mascot stood, pumping up the crowd, and was barking at him furiously, which was fair enough.

It was chaos. It was gold.

And Benji was nearing the finish line, where Jess waited, her hands outstretched.

"And with Thumper definitely out," the announcer called, "and George the bulldog now trying to gnaw our mascot, we have one pooch heading for the prize, and that's Tom Chavez's Benji. And yes! He's crossed the finish line first!"

Benji plowed into Jess, sending her sprawling on her backside on the ice. But she was laughing, as Benji licked her face.

"Woohoo!" Tom cheered and skated to where Jess was hugging Benji, as Bree clapped nearby, a huge grin on her face.

"We did it!"

He dropped to his knees and hugged Benji as a TV camera swooped in. He lifted one of Benji's paws and waved at the camera. "Yay!"

"Let's get a shot of the three of you." The cameraman asked them to huddle together.

He drew Jess close, Benji between them, and wrapped his arm around her.

Her laughter faded, her expression growing shy as she looked at him.

"Look at the camera," the team's media guy instructed.

"Uh, sure." Jess smile held nervousness, which was fair enough. This was the part of the show they hadn't practiced.

Around them, other dogs were finishing their runs, some clearly giving up, to their various owners' laughter or bemused resignation.

An uproar from the sides drew their attention where George-the-bulldog was now urinating on the mascot, Harvey the Hound.

"Quick, get some footage of that!" The media guy pointed to the cameraman.

"I don't think that George the bulldog's Mom was wearing enough red," Tom smirked.

Jess laughed, and he was glad he remembered her joke from before.

The interviewer returned, and directed the cameraman their way again. "So, Tom, tell us about your prize winner of a pooch here." The interviewer thrust a microphone at Tom.

"This is Benji, who was originally my sister's dog, until he came to live with me earlier this year when she became a mom. He's a golden Labrador, and just the best dog companion."

"And your dog's mom?" The interviewer held the micro-phone to Jess.

She glanced at Tom, and he gave her an encouraging nod.

"I'm Jess, and I agree that Benji is a beautiful boy. Very sweet natured."

"And she's a vet, J. James Veterinary Practice," Tom added. "So if you want excellent pet care, then look her up on the inter-net." On her brand new website which Cassie and Poppy had helped her set up and had been published online just yesterday.

"Some might call that an unfair advantage, having a girlfriend who is a vet." The interviewer smiled. "I have a feeling you might not be allowed to participate next year."

"I know that anyone who has Dr. Jess care for their pet will be blessed and glad that she's in their life. I know I am." He looked across, saw her cheeks had pinked. He smiled.

"Aww, you three make the cutest little family. Congratula-tions, Benji."

And Benji, like the media star he was obviously destined to be, gave an enormous woof.

THE REST of the day passed in a blur, her heart snagged by Tom's words.

He hadn't denied she was his girlfriend. In fact, the rest of the time, as he casually slung an arm around her, even kissed her cheek a time or two, he seemed intent on showing they were in some kind of relationship when they clearly weren't.

So while this was fun, and she hadn't laughed as much as she had in years, concern and uncertainty still bubbled away, making her antsy as he drove her home.

"So, did you have fun?" he asked.

"It was so much fun. I haven't laughed as much as that in years."

"We all need more laughter in this world."

And he brought joy and laughter to her world. She glanced across. "Thank you for your mention of the vet practice."

He chuckled. "I suspect some people might've thought I was pushing it a little too much, but I don't care. I'm just glad you got a few potential clients from it."

Five of the players or the team's personnel had spoken with her, asking for her to check over their pet. And her phone had a dozen emails from her brand new website's email address, which all looked to be inquiries.

"I can't believe that a brief plug today has seen so much interest."

He peeked across. "Obviously everyone could tell that you're a high caliber kind of vet. I might've mentioned to a few of the others that you do dog training too. I hope that's okay."

"Sure."

"It's obvious that some of those dogs need you."

She chuckled again. "I don't know if I'm allowed to admit this, but it was funny to see George piddle on the mascot."

He laughed too. "He's going to be a lot more careful about what he says to rev up the crowd from now on. No more jokes about bulldogs."

"It was good to see they raised so much money for the kids' charity."

"I love that about our sport. It's so focused on others."

They fell into silence, but she still felt itchy, nervous. Talking about Benji and her career was awesome, but what had he meant by ignoring the interviewer's comment about Jess being Tom's girlfriend? How could she ask about that? *Lord?*

Be brave. "Um, I hope people aren't too worried about what the interviewer said."

"What part?" He peered across briefly, then returned his attention to the road.

She swallowed. "About... about me being your..."

"My vet? I wouldn't worry about it."

"No." She cleared her throat, then whispered, "about being your girlfriend."

His chin dipped, and he peered across at her again, then refocused on the road as he slowed at an intersection.

Silence filled the interior, apart from Benji's snores. Clearly today's activity had worn him out.

Trees passed, snow lay on the ground, as she wondered what to do. She'd spoken up, which had felt brave, but now it felt like a risk too far.

Finally he sighed. "I didn't realize it was a problem."

Huh? "It's not. Except... it's not exactly true." It wasn't true at *all*. Apart from the fact that she was a girl and she was his friend.

His fingers drummed on the steering wheel. "Look, I figured it didn't matter too much, and that we both know the truth, so we should just let it slide."

It didn't matter? Why? Because he didn't care? Her heart twisted with a savage pang. Oh, clearly her mom was wrong and Jess had misunderstood everything if he said it didn't matter. Did he mean he didn't care whether people thought they were a couple or not, because he clearly didn't think they were? If so, what did *that* mean? Had he only been using her to look after his dog?

She faced out the window, her eyes blurring.

"Jess?"

"Mm?"

"Is something wrong?"

Plenty of things felt wrong right now. Starting with her ability to read a man. How could she have let herself be used by an untrustworthy man again? How could she have been so naive?

"You're really quiet."

"I'm kind of tired." Tired of getting things wrong, tired of being hurt by people. She wanted to crawl into a ball and hide, not play pretend with this man whose overly affectionate ways had led her to believe that he cared.

"Have I said something wrong? If I have, I'm sorry."

She clamped her lips to stop a protest from leaking. See, this was why she had fallen for this man. How could she not when he said sweet things like that? But clearly he didn't want her. He didn't *want* her.

She pressed her knuckles to her forehead. "Sorry. I've got a headache." It now wasn't a lie. The space felt too close, the comment before about the three of them being a family only reminded her that they weren't, and this wasn't her car, wasn't her life, wasn't her reality.

So when they arrived at the ranch, she took Benji to his bed, and didn't let Tom touch her in one of his hugs or cheek kisses that he'd so carelessly bestowed before. Didn't he know those kinds of things meant something to a girl?

He shuffled awkwardly. "Well, uh, thanks again."

"Sure."

"I hope you get lots of clients."

"I appreciate your efforts to help."

His forehead wrinkled. "Jess, have I done something wrong? This feels weird."

How could she admit out loud that she was upset because he didn't want her as a girlfriend? Those words would never escape her lips. "I don't feel great right now. Sorry."

His face softened with compassion. "I know it's been a big day. I'll be praying for you."

She nodded, and didn't respond like she usually did with an "I'll be praying for you too." Nope. Couldn't say it. Even though she'd probably still do it. "I need to go."

"Okay."

And he nodded, took a step forward as if to hug her, but she stepped back. No, she would not succumb to his charm.

"Right. Bye Benji." He crouched and rubbed the dog's head, then stood and faced her again. "Okay, I'll see you in a week."

She nodded, but couldn't speak. The boulder-sized lump in her throat refused to let her talk. She'd make sure that would be a clinical handover. Maybe she'd even ask Mom to do it, like the brave person she was trying to be these days.

She found half a smile, and braced herself on the door and watched him reverse then drive away.

Then, when her mom came in and asked how it went, the emotion welled up and spilled out along with the oh-so-painful truth.

That Tom didn't want her. That he'd only ever wanted her to be the vet for his dog. And that contrary to both of their hopes and expectations, she was never going to share a future with the man she'd finally realized would be perfect in hers.

The one whose vehicle's tail-lights had disappeared into the night.

Seventeen

Tom might possess skills on ice, but clearly he lacked them with women. He couldn't get Jess's strange reaction out of his mind, even as they embarked on a mid-November road trip that saw them take in cities from Dallas, Tampa Bay and Nashville.

He might've scored points in each of those games, but he almost didn't care when he returned and Jess dropped off Benji with barely a word, let alone a glance.

"How have you been?"

"Busy."

"Got some new clients?"

"Yep. Sorry, gotta run."

She'd ruffled Benji and then left without sparing Tom another look. Huh. He'd clearly lost points with Jess. But for what he didn't know.

He was prepared to put it down to busyness—that must be why she hadn't replied to his messages—but then the same thing happened when he dropped Benji back at the ranch before an early December trip east. Leonie, Derek and Cassie were happy to talk, Jess not so much.

"Sorry, I've got a bunch of paperwork to do."

"But Jess," Leonie protested, "he's heading away tomorrow —"

"Sorry, this can't wait."

Her gaze flicked to his and the hurt there wrung his heart. Had someone upset her? *Was* it him? But she refused to answer.

He'd figured to surprise her when he returned from that road trip and finally make her talk. But when he pulled up at the ranch she wasn't there, so he was left floundering with Derek, who didn't seem to suspect anything was wrong with his daughter, even though Tom had asked.

"I think she's tired. Going from all that work to none to learning to get back in the saddle so to speak is challenging. And she's got those same workaholic tendencies that all my children do, so it's hard for her to say no, especially when she can see animals in need."

He'd frowned. "She's still only working three days, right? I thought that was what she agreed to."

Derek scratched his chin. "She might be doing three and a half. Apparently there were a lot of inquiries."

He felt a throb of concern. "She needs to be careful to not overdo it."

"I think she's really happy to be getting back into doing something."

But there still seemed a sense of strain, something evident by the way she barely responded to his messages. Was she feeling depressed again? Derek hadn't mentioned that, so maybe not. Or maybe that just meant Jess had gotten better at hiding her symptoms.

He couldn't help but be grateful that Franklin seemed clueless, clearly distracted by something else, acting like a bit of a bear. But Tom didn't mind as it wasn't directed at him, which made a nice change. But without Franklin as a source for intel, who could he ask?

He worried it over as they returned from a trip to Pittsburg and St. Paul to Canadian airspace. Winnipeg was the last stop before their return. His heart thudded. And Winnipeg was where Jess's sister, Poppy, lived. Maybe this was a chance to find out more.

"Thanks for meeting me."

Poppy looked up from her cup of chai and delicately blew on the steaming liquid. "I was surprised to get a message from you. I didn't know you had my number."

It had taken some doing. He wasn't going to ask Jess or Cassie for their sister's number—that wouldn't look shady at all. So instead he'd asked Winnipeg's NHL captain Luc Blanchard to ask Bailey to pass on a message that he'd like to talk to Poppy. Which had been an even more roundabout way of finding out what he wanted to know, and likely raised even more flags about his interest in Jess. But still, it was done now, and now he was here, sitting in the Coffee Haus coffee shop which seemed anything but homey with its stark industrial walls and vibe.

He took a sip then almost choked on his too-hot coffee. He had thirty minutes before he needed to rejoin the team for the bus ride to the arena. "I wanted to ask about Jess."

"Did you now?"

Okay, this didn't look good. Poppy's reputation for straight talking blew even Cassie and Jess's out of the water.

Her eyes narrowed. "What exactly is it you want to know about my sister?"

Time to man up. Here went nothing. "Do you know why she is avoiding me?"

"How exactly is she avoiding you?"

"Not answering my texts. She's barely spoken a dozen words to me. And now we're nearing Christmas and I hate to have this hanging over me, especially when I don't know what I've done wrong."

"Oh, you disappoint me, Tom."

"Excuse me?"

"Typical man, thinking it's all about him."

"I asked your dad and he doesn't think there's anything the matter."

"That's because he's not privy to the sister chat."

"What's the sister chat?"

"Cassie, Jess and I have started a sister chat."

"Has Jess said something there about what's wrong?"

Poppy's delicate fingers played on the handle of her cup. Dancer fingers, thin and elegant. "Do you like my sister?"

"Of course I do."

"No, I mean *like* her. As in you care about her and want to go out with her and date her and be boyfriend / girlfriend and all that happy-happy joy-joy stuff?" She rolled her eyes.

Wow. Who had made her so cynical? Her brows arched. She was waiting for an answer. "You know I do."

"You do? Seriously?"

"What do you think I've been doing the past eighteen months?" Frustration leaked. "I've been working my guts out just to get her to notice me, then she was too busy, then she had her breakdown, and since then I've been working to get her to trust me."

Her eyes slitted. "Are you saying you did all of this stuff with Benji simply so she would notice you?"

Put like that it sounded awful. "It seemed to be the only way for her to see me," he mumbled.

"Oh my gosh. Men are so unbelievable! Actually, no. That's completely believable, knowing the kinds of men I've known. Do you know how manipulative that sounds?"

"Hey, no," he said firmly. "I was *never* manipulative. I really thought we'd hit it off. But then she just withdrew after the dog run on ice event."

"The time when she was referred to as your girlfriend?"

He nodded, thinking back. That's right. Jess had raised that in the car on the return journey. But he hadn't paid attention, just tried to laugh it off.

"She asked me about it later," he admitted. "I didn't want her to feel pressured so I didn't say anything. I've never tried to make her do anything she doesn't want."

She folded her arms, her eyes arctic and stormy. "Now you're making me want to hurt you."

"Huh?"

"I don't like how that sounds. You are hardly making me feel like you've been treating my sister with the respect she deserves."

"What?" Then he realized how his earlier words might be misconstrued. "No. No *way*. I haven't even kissed her let alone done anything else like you're suggesting. Just no. I actually can't believe you'd even think something like that about me. That's offensive."

"Well, okay then. Maybe I was wrong."

"Maybe? You're *definitely* wrong. I don't know who's hurt you and is now living rent-free in your head, but I'm not that kind of guy. I've only ever wanted the best for her. And you should know that by now."

She eyed him, her chin mutinous still. Then she lowered it. "You haven't even kissed her?"

"A couple of times on the cheek, but that's it."

"Lame," she muttered.

Whoa. This woman might be a dancer, but she had him tiptoeing like eggshells had cracked aplenty. "What do you mean by that?"

"If you like her then you need to tell her. But leaving her in this place of not knowing isn't fair. You can't laugh off a 'she's your girlfriend' joke and not expect it to eat at her. Especially if —" She clamped her lips.

"Especially if what?"

She exhaled. "I don't know why I need to spell it out. I really thought you were smarter than this. But here goes: if she didn't feel something, she wouldn't be upset, would she?"

He tried to untangle that. Wait... "You mean she does feel something for me, so that's why she's upset?"

"Oh my gosh. I can't deal with this." She pushed back her seat. Stood. "You are paying for my chai, and then you have a bus to catch. And then, when you get home, you have some groveling to do."

"I appreciate your time."

"I'd appreciate it if you fixed things with my sister so she's happy again."

"I'll do my best." He offered a weak smile. "Might need you to pray, seeing my best isn't very good."

"Oh, I will." Her severe expression relaxed. "Now, are you coming to our place for Christmas?"

He hadn't been invited, so, "No."

"Why not? That would be the perfect time to make things up to her. I'll invite you if nobody else has."

"I think my folks were planning to do something in Regina. It's my niece's first Christmas."

"Oh, that's special." She bit her lip, her face softening a little more. Maybe babies were a key to her heart. "Okay, but you do need to find a way to talk to Jess and let her know how you feel, and I wouldn't leave it too long. My sister might be the smartest of us all, but she can be pretty dumb about things sometimes too. Which is why you two probably would make a good pair," she added snidely.

"You need to watch yourself." He pointed. "I'm going to pray for you too that you find some guy who knocks off all your hard edges."

"Yeah, good luck with that."

"Don't need good luck. Just need God."

She snickered. Opened her arms. "Come here."

He was getting a hug now? Not from the James sister he wanted, but still, he'd take acceptance from someone in the family.

"You need to be clear with her, okay?" she murmured as he hugged her. "No more beating around the bush. If you want her, go and get her. Just let her know that you care." She pulled back, grinned. "So, go get her, cowboy."

"Yes, ma'am."

Ｄｅｃｅｍｂｅｒ ｄｒｉｆｔｅｄ by in a busy clutter of Jess's new clients and jobs, yet was underscored by disappointment.

Yes, it had been childish to ignore Tom's messages, to avoid him when it came to handing over Benji, but her heart felt fragile, like she couldn't trust herself to try again and have her hopes fail. There'd been too much of that already this year, and wallowing in the what ifs and maybes wasn't healthy for her. She knew that only too well. It was far better to completely avoid the man and not be forced to think about him. Even if Mom and Dad still insisted on asking about him, and Cassie and Harrison asked after him all the time.

The last time she'd seen Tom he'd been less insistent on speaking to her, a little kinder, so she'd wondered if he'd given up. Which was good. Just what she wanted. And must be why he wasn't here for Christmas, even though she knew Mom had invited him. She'd overheard them the last time he'd called by. An unscheduled visit, not to pick up or drop off Benji, but just because.

She'd overheard them while hiding in her room—real mature—but she'd been wearing a green avocado facial mask Poppy had sent her that was supposed to make her skin feel amazing. After a long week she'd only just hopped into her pajamas, and really wasn't up to changing just because a man thought he'd take it upon himself to drop by unannounced. So she'd stayed hidden, heard Mom invite him to Christmas, and yelled a silent *No, no, no.* Then heard his regrets and refusal which had scored a silent *Yes.*

And now, here she was on Christmas Day, sitting in the living room while Mom finished making the gravy, watching the happy couples around her, wishing she was one of them.

Poppy kept looking at the door. "Is Tom not coming?"

"Nope. That's why Benji is here." She pointed to where Benji was entertaining Hannah's mom, who was seated on the sofa near the Christmas tree.

"Oh." Poppy frowned.

Her sister's disappointment compounded her own, making her punchy. "Why would he? He's not family. He's got his own."

"I just really thought he would." She shook her head. "Wow, that man is a disappointment."

Oh, her heart must be really messed up if she got offended by that. Yes, Tom had disappointed her, but she still didn't want anyone else to say that out loud. Blood might be thicker than water, but it somehow still felt like her heart was connected to his. And even though he'd let her down, it felt disloyal to say that out loud. Or let anyone else's negative comments about him to remain unchallenged. "That's harsh."

Poppy eyed her, her blue-green eyes piercing in a way that gave her beautiful features a hard edge. "Did you ever talk things out with him?"

"No. There's nothing to talk about."

"Please." Poppy scoffed. "You like him and he likes you and you're still upset, so yeah. You two have plenty to talk about."

"He doesn't like me."

"How many times has that man tried to contact you? No, seriously. Where's your phone?" Poppy snatched up Jess's phone.

"Hey!" Jess tried to grab it, but Poppy held it out of reach.

Poppy waved it in front of Jess's face so it unlocked, then started scrolling.

"Oh my gosh, Jess! Look at all these unanswered calls. You're insane if you think the man doesn't care."

"What happened to him being such a disappointment?"

"That was until I realized my sister is being an even bigger one. You can't bury your head in the sand and blame a man for not trying to connect when clearly he has been!"

"Keep your voice down."

"Fine." Poppy muttered. "I wasn't going to tell you this, but —"

"It's ready!" Mom called. "Girls, come and help serve, please."

"But what?" Jess poked Poppy as they moved to the kitchen. "You can't begin a sentence like that and leave me hanging."

Poppy smiled with her fake sweet smile. "Oh yes I can."

"Grr."

"Careful. You'll make Benji jealous."

Jess swallowed and faked a smile for Mom, but her sister's words rankled. Why was she still looking after that man's dog when he didn't care? Although maybe Poppy was right, and she should've made more of an effort. Okay, any effort. Instead, she'd turned her back on him, letting her fears get in the way of a possible future, yet again. That was hardly the way a believer should behave, holding unforgiveness and offense, letting it snarl her heart into a tangled mess of emotion. Her eyes prickled with heat.

"Excuse me a minute." She rushed to the laundry, and gripped the sink, Benji trotting after her like he sensed she was upset. She snuggled into him, her tears seeping into his hair. Then closed her eyes. "Lord, I'm sorry. I haven't been living like You want me to. Please forgive me." Her heart hurt. "Cleanse out all this gunk in my heart. And I know it's Christmas, but I'd really like to feel hope again and not carry this hurt into the new year."

She drew in a breath. Released. Drew in another. Wiped her face.

"Jess?" Cassie's voice. "Are you in here?"

She blinked hard, rose, and dusted off a few stray Benji hairs from her black pants. "I'm just checking on the drinks situation." She pulled open the door of the spare fridge. "Yep. Plenty here."

"O-kay...." Cassie sounded unsure. "We're almost all dished up. You better hurry if you don't want Franklin to eat it all."

"We can't have that, can we?"

She rejoined the others in the kitchen, served herself some

turkey, potatoes, sweet potatoes, then took her place beside Hannah, opposite Poppy.

Dad prayed a blessing over their meal, then they dug in. The food was good, but she kept chewing on what Poppy might've been about to say. Had Poppy spoken to Tom? That would be just like her to do that and not tell her. That would actually make sense too, with her 'I wasn't going to tell you' comment. And she wouldn't leave her hanging unless it was good news, right? But wasn't this to-ing and fro-ing just more of the seesaw of confusing emotions she couldn't live with anymore? *Lord, I need You to help me. I give You all of this.*

Her heart settled, and she re-tuned into the conversations around her. The couples were seated together, Harrison and Cassie next to Poppy, and Hannah's mom on Poppy's other side. Franklin and Hannah sat next to Jess, with an empty seat on the other side of her. Hannah wasn't eating much, and Harrison kept grinning at Cassie, like they had a secret.

"Are you feeling okay?" she murmured to Hannah.

Now she looked at her, her sister-in-law wasn't looking radiant as she had a few weeks ago. Hannah glanced at her, and Jess caught a glimmer of tears. "Oh, Han. What is it?"

"I can't talk about it here."

She reached across and gently squeezed her sister-in-law's hand. Franklin noticed, and placed his hand on Hannah's knee. How long had Hannah been feeling like this? She rarely showed emotion publicly, having been trained in the art of professional speaking as part of her journalist career. Had Jess been so lost in her own troubles she'd been blind to other people's?

Harrison cleared his throat. "Well, I'm glad we're all here, for we have an announcement."

One guess what that would be.

Cassie held up her left hand, which wore a huge diamond ring. "Harrison asked me to marry him and I said yes!"

Among the squeals of excitement, Jess felt a throb of pain. Not that she was missing out, but because she'd made choices that meant the man she loved wasn't here. She could have spoken to him several times. Could have answered his calls, his texts. But instead, she'd let stubborn pride keep her from someone who had continually tried to reach out.

The celebrations continued with Hannah's mom proposing a toast. "All of your fans will be so disappointed."

"I don't care," Harrison declared, gazing at Cassie with eyes of love. "I'm marrying the woman of my dreams and that's enough for me."

Jess's heart tipped again. She loved her sister, but sometimes it seemed crazy to think a Hollywood actor would love her sister the way he clearly did. The mystery of love. It must explain why some people got together, and others let it pass them by. Of course, then there were those who were simply too blind or prideful to recognize it when it basically came and lay at her feet and begged, wishing for a rub on the tummy.

Hannah quietly excused herself, and Franklin moved to follow but she refused him. "I'm fine."

She clearly wasn't.

"Are you sure my daughter is okay, Franklin?" Hannah's mom asked. "Perhaps I'll go check on her."

"No, I'll go." Jess stood and hurried after Hannah, finding her upstairs on Franklin's old bed, lying down. "Han?"

She moved around, saw the tears staining her cheeks, knelt beside the bed. "What's happened?"

Hannah's breath hitched. "I... I had a miscarriage a few days ago."

Her chest panged. "Oh, Han. I'm so sorry."

"I didn't realize I wanted it until now. Franklin was excited, but I just wanted my career. And now..." She shuddered. "Now I've lost a child. And I am glad for Cassie, but it also kind of hurts to see someone else be happy when I feel like my heart is breaking."

She understood that only too well. She'd felt exactly like that during those weeks of wanting to hide in darkness while outside summer blazed. She stroked Hannah's arm, passing her some tissues from the box beside the bed. "Hey, you don't need to stay. I'll even drive you home if you want. People will understand."

"My mom won't." Hannah blew her nose. "She's always drilled into me the importance of chasing my career, which is what I always thought I wanted. Except then I got pregnant, which was a real shock, and then," her voice broke on a sob, "I lost the baby. And now, I just don't know. Everything I thought I wanted has changed."

"Oh, Han." She leaned close, wrapped her arms around her and hugged her. "And yet, God is here in the midst of it. This hasn't taken Him by surprise."

Hannah's tears soaked through the shoulder of Jess's top. "I know. It just hurts."

"Do you want me to get Franklin?"

"No." Hannah sniffled. "He's been struggling with this too. I think he'd love to be a dad, and this has really rocked him."

A floorboard groaned, and Jess looked up to see Franklin standing at the door. "You'll both be in my prayers."

"Thanks." Hannah drew in a deep breath as Franklin drew near.

He gently gripped Jess's shoulder, and she hugged him then left the two of them together, and moved to the bathroom to fix her makeup. Poor Hannah. Poor Franklin. How hard this must be.

But also, a tiny voice whispered, *what an important reminder.* That life had unexpected detours, and things might not always work out the way one intended. But if a person remembered that God was with them, then they could be assured He would always navigate them aright, and lead them into paths of blessing. Even those people who had been blind to what they thought they wanted.

She shuddered out a breath and returned downstairs.

Then froze at the sight of the man who now sat at the table.

Eighteen

This was a bad idea. He'd thought that taking Poppy's advice and surprising Jess by leaving his family's Christmas then coming here would be something she'd appreciate. Turned out that surprises weren't his forte.

Leonie had welcomed him in—he'd needed to check it was okay with her—but the atmosphere was strained. Franklin and Hannah weren't here, neither was the woman he'd come to see, yet Cassie and Harrison looked pleased as punch. He gathered they'd gotten recently engaged, so he congratulated them, but otherwise things felt awkward.

Poppy's attention shifted behind him, and the way she quickly glanced back at him meant it could only be one person.

He turned. Smiled. "Hey Jess. Merry Christmas."

She blinked. "M-merry Christmas to you too." She hesitated, looking at where Poppy had drawn up a chair, insisting he sit there. Right next to where Jess had been sitting, it seemed. "I... I didn't know you were coming."

"Your mom invited me."

She slipped into her seat and Benji—until then, his head happily on Tom's lap—put his head on hers instead. Traitor.

Her family looked at them, then as one turned to Cassie and Harrison and began discussing wedding plans.

"I thought you couldn't come," she murmured, as Poppy pretended not to eavesdrop.

"Turned out I could come, after all."

"Didn't you see your family?"

"I did. Then I caught a plane and came here."

"What—today?"

"Yep. I got in just over an hour ago and came straight here."

Her eyes were huge, and he could see the questions in them. And suddenly wished they weren't on public display. That instead of agreeing to sit down and make awkward conversation for the past fifteen minutes he'd found a way to insist on waiting to speak with Jess privately.

He *really* wished to speak with her alone.

"Hey Tom," Poppy said, "I think you should call your next dog Peeve."

"Why?"

"Because then you can tell everyone 'This is my pet Peeve'."

He chuckled, and caught Jess's small smile.

"Hey, I've got one," Cassie said. "You can lead a horse to water, but you can't make it lasso."

"Oh, honey, that was bad," Harrison chuckled.

"As bad as Poppy's?"

"Not quite as bad as Poppy's."

"Hey!" Poppy mock-frowned.

Leonie stood. "Well, seeing Hannah and Franklin are still gone, how about we clear these plates and get ready for dessert?"

Dessert. He liked the sound of that.

Jess shifted as if to help, and her mom stopped her.

"No, Jess, you and Tom need to catch up, especially seeing he's just flown all this way to see you."

Jess bit her lip. Peeked up at him.

He nodded.

"Actually, why don't you take him to the barn?" Cassie

suggested. "Miranda has had some kittens and they need to be checked. Preferably by an expert."

"But—"

"But nothing," Poppy said. "Tom, you want to see kittens, don't you?"

There was only one answer, and that was, "Absolutely."

Both sisters smiled at him, then at each other, then at Jess, who clearly knew her role too. "Fine. We'll be a minute."

"Take as long as you need," Leonie called.

"Oh my gosh." Jess fanned her pink face. "My family is so embarrassing."

They could be as embarrassing as they liked for all he cared. Cutting time short with his own family to be here suddenly seemed very worthwhile.

He followed Jess to the mud room off the laundry, waiting as she slipped into boots. She eyed his shoes, the warmest sneakers he owned that he hadn't had time to change from since getting off the plane. "You might find them slippery on the snow."

"I'm used to walking on ice. How warm is the barn?"

"It's not exactly a sauna."

"Good. I don't like things getting too hot."

Her lips twitched, and he realized what he'd said. Which wasn't intentional and didn't sound especially appropriate on Christmas Day. "I meant—oh, forget it."

"Come on."

They trudged across the snowy path to the barn and she opened the door to an office area.

"Your cat sleeps in here?" he asked, looking around at the desks and shelves.

"No, but this door is easier to open than the big barn door."

"Fair enough."

But—why were they talking about barn doors when he had far more important things to talk about? He followed her from the office into the main barn area.

She moved to the hayloft and climbed the ladder. "Hello, Miranda. How are you and your babies?"

Oh, so there really were cats, and this wasn't just some elaborate plot of the sisters to get him alone with Jess.

She peered down at him. "Want to see them?"

"Sure." He gestured to the ladder. "Is it safe for me to climb that thing?"

"If it can hold Franklin, I'm sure it'll hold you too."

"Okay."

He followed her up and met Miranda the cat and her kittens. Jess tugged off her gloves and handled them, checking them over, Miranda watching her intently. Jess gently stroked her, her care and compassion evident, then glanced at him, uncertainty in every feature.

"You know, Jess, I actually didn't come here to see the cat. I came to see you."

She ducked her head, and her uncertainty seemed to ripple through him.

Lord, what will it take for her to trust me?

LORD, help me to be brave enough to trust him with the truth.

It still seemed surreal that Tom was here. Sitting in the hayloft, as if he didn't have a care in the world. But she couldn't be so blithe. The challenge presented by Hannah earlier only reminded her of what she needed to do. To be brave. To have faith. To trust God.

"Um, did you want to stay up here? Or go somewhere else?"

"I'm happy wherever you are."

Oh, that could be a line in a cheesy Hallmark film, but the serious look in his eye—so different to the usual joker she knew—made her almost dare to believe him. And perhaps on this day that celebrated when a Savior had been born she could trust her Savior to have His way in all that occurred.

"I'd rather talk down there." She pointed down below.

"Okay."

She descended slowly, brushing the hay off her as she looked around for a place to sit.

He motioned to a couple of hay bales. "Like we're in a stable. Appropriate for Christmas Day, huh?"

She sat, and he lowered himself to the other one. She had to find the right words, but all the speeches she'd imagined refused to fall into place. She looked up at him, saw his attention on her still. Found a small smile. "Thank you for coming today."

"I wasn't sure you'd want me to."

She ducked her head. "I'm sorry. I've been a bit of a mess lately."

"Hey, it's okay."

"It's not." She met his gaze. His green eyes seemed so much darker in the barn's dimness. "I'm sorry for ghosting you."

"You didn't quite ghost me. I seem to recall a couple of messages." His gaze was sober. "But I hope you know that I never meant to hurt you."

How could she have treated him so badly, when he'd been nothing but her friend? Her heart wavered. Was this a mistake? Had she misread things again? But then, why would he have cut Christmas with his own family short to come see her if he didn't care for her, at least a little bit?

Time to own the truth. "I," she swallowed, moisture was lacking. "I guess I was confused after the charity day when you said you didn't want me to be your girlfriend. I... I thought you cared."

"Wait—I didn't say I didn't want you as my girlfriend. Did I?"

"That's what I heard. I thought you said it didn't matter what others thought, that they could think," she took a breath, "that we were together but it wasn't true so it didn't matter."

"Jess, no. I didn't mean that to sound like that at all." He grasped her hand, the touch of his fingers as they tangled in hers drawing fire like they had before. "I'm so sorry it sounded like that."

"So what did you mean?"

"I meant that I didn't want you feeling like I'd placed you in an awkward position where people assumed things that you maybe weren't ready for."

"Like what?"

His Adam's apple dipped. "Like being my girlfriend."

His words, the rasp in his voice, that intent look in his eye, sawed through the last of her uncertainty. It was time to be brave.

She stood, tugged him upright. "Do you remember when we danced together at Franklin's wedding?"

He stilled. Then dipped his chin. "Yes."

She cringed inside. That hardly sounded like he'd enjoyed it. Seriously, what was she saying this for? He was still watching her. She had to say something. "You're a, uh, good height to dance with." She could die. That was the best she could do? "Especially when I'm wearing heels."

His lips tweaked. "Or boots like this." His foot nudged the toe of her cowboy boot.

Nerves skittered inside.

"Are you saying you want to dance again?" His voice was low, husky.

"With you?" she dared.

His eyes bored into hers. "Yes."

"Then yes."

Tom's eyes glinted, then he held out his hand, and she placed hers in his. And just like before it seemed they magically fit. Just like when they hugged. They fit together, perfectly.

He drew her close. "We don't have music."

"Are you sure about that?" she murmured, resting her face against his neck.

His skin was warm, and she closed her eyes as they gently swayed. This wasn't the dance of friends, but one of two people who liked each other. A lot.

She moved her face, curling into his neck a little more, breathing in his skin. Cool Water. A scent that sent tingles to her toes.

His arm stole around her back, drawing her closer still. Her hand held by his, gently, reverently, still arced fire between them.

Her lips grazed his neck, and he stilled.

"Jess?" he murmured.

"Mm?"

"Do you remember when we danced before?"

"Yes." Although they hadn't stood as close as this.

"I wanted you to be my girlfriend then."

Her head tipped back, her eyes searching his. "You did? Eighteen months ago?"

"Yes." His lips half curved. "I didn't realize then just what lengths I'd have to go to show you I was serious."

"Are you joking?"

His eyes darkened. "I couldn't joke about things like this. Not with you."

His head lowered, lowered some more, then his breath whispered against her skin. "This is no joke."

Then his lips gently grazed hers.

Oh, the stars that ignited within. Wondrous, white twinkly points of light.

Her hand slid to curve around his neck, and she pressed in more eagerly.

His arm stole around her waist and he held her as she leaned in, exploring the softness of his mouth, sighing at the pleasure of it all.

His mouth fell to the side of hers and he kissed the corner of her lips, one side, then the other. Then his mouth returned to where it was meant to be, his other hand cupping the back of her head as he kissed and he kissed and he kissed her.

She didn't want him to stop. She could drown in this feeling of delirious delight.

Until an overhead light flicked on, flooding the space with

brightness, and Benji bounded in, breaking the moment with hearty woofs as if relieved to find them.

She stumbled back, her lips swollen, sure her hair was a mess too.

Poppy smirked at the door. "Well, well, well. I came to tell you dessert is ready but it looks like some people have decided to have dessert early."

"Go away Poppy."

"Can't. Your presence is required. Yours too." She nodded to Tom. "Good job, by the way."

"Thanks."

"Good job?"

"I might've seen him in Winnipeg and told him to tell you how he feels. Looks like someone here was paying attention and did exactly that."

He chuckled, and wrapped an arm around Jess's waist. "I'm glad you helped me see the light."

"You're welcome. Now Jess, can you tell me what's wrong with Hannah?"

The wondrous glory of moments earlier dissipated at the memory of Hannah and Franklin's distress. This was their news to tell. "Have they said anything?"

Poppy shook her head. "Franklin came downstairs not long after you left and said Hannah was unwell and they had to go home. He also said he'd like you to tell us what Hannah said."

She sighed. "Hannah had a miscarriage."

Poppy gasped, her hands over her mouth. "Oh no."

"Man." Tom blew out a breath. "Poor Franklin. I knew he'd been a bit off lately."

"I don't know if Hannah's mom knew, but I think Mom suspected. She'll be devastated."

"Maybe don't make an announcement then," Poppy said. "You could share that privately, and make a different announcement instead."

Tom tugged Jess a little closer. "What kind of announcement would you like that to be?"

Her heart startled, her mind leaping ahead to all kinds of announcements he might mean.

His lips quirked, his eyes laughing, as he drew a finger down her cheek. "How about we start with saying we're dating?"

"Okay. That sounds like a plan."

"Dating is a good start for something more, anyway." Poppy said, before sashaying out.

He smiled, and Jess let him steal another kiss, then another along her jaw. "We should go."

"I'd really like to stay."

"Me too. But it seems like we might be needed inside."

"As long as you know I need you by my side," he murmured against her jaw.

Mmm. She was starting to get that idea.

Nineteen

The seven weeks since Christmas had seen twenty-two games, fourteen wins and eight losses. He'd scored five goals, ten assists, and been the game's third star two times. But more importantly, he'd gained one girlfriend, and collected one hundred percent of her kisses. And it seemed that kissing was a new hobby of this clever veterinarian, who was more than happy to oblige him whenever he called by.

And now, on Valentine's Day, he had a little something to give her. It wasn't that little, but seeing he'd not given her a Christmas gift, he'd thought to make the most of it now.

She met him at his condo, leading Benji, who wore a red bow tie and sparkly vest that looked like something Poppy might have suggested.

He laughed. "Who did that to my dog?"

"Whose dog?" she challenged, smirking.

"Our dog," he corrected. "But come on. All he needs is a rhinestone cowboy hat to complete that look."

"Poppy sent it over."

"I knew it. Man. I really hope poor Benji hasn't seen himself in a mirror. He'd be so embarrassed."

She laughed, and kissed him. "Now behave."

"But it's Valentine's Day. And you..." The skirt of her red dress swung as he twirled her out then in. "You look so beautiful."

She laughed, spinning back and coming to rest with her hand on his chest. "You don't look too bad yourself. I like you in a suit."

"I tried."

He bent and kissed her, their passion quickly growing until Benji woofed.

"Oops. Looks like our chaperone dog is on the job."

She fanned herself. "Looks like he needs to. You kiss a little too well."

"I can stop if that helps."

"That would not help at all. This vet needs her Valentine."

"And this Valentine needs his vet."

She laughed. "Are you saying Benji is my Valentine?"

"I'm your Valentine," he said firmly, and proved it with a kiss that soon earned another disapproving woof.

"Come on. We'll be late."

Jess had decided to surprise him by arranging a date for Valentine's Day, which was very liberated of her. But the fact she'd dressed up meant she must have similar ideas to him on what kind of date this could be. Except... "Is Benji coming?"

"Is that a problem? I just figured he might enjoy the evening out."

"But we could enjoy it more without him."

"I'm not sure I want to know what you mean by that."

"I think," he nuzzled her neck, "you could get the idea pretty quickly, especially as you're so smart."

She chuckled and pushed him away. "I appreciate your enthusiasm, but I'm not going to go there until I'm like Hannah with a couple of rings on my finger."

"Hey, I just meant the tower restaurant. I don't think they let dogs in there."

"Oh." She blushed. "I didn't mean to imply anything."

He kissed her nose. "You're too easy to tease."

"Then stop taking advantage of me, and let's go."

He got Benji in the back of her car and opened the driver's door for her. "I presume you're going to drive."

"You presume correctly. Now get in and let's go."

She drove to a dog friendly restaurant, and they were escorted to a room at the back with only a few couples. It seemed they were the only ones who'd brought a pet pooch, but he couldn't mind too much. Not when Benji had done so much to bring them together.

Their waiter left, and Jess smiled at him. "See? This is nice, isn't it?"

"This is very nice." He kissed her, his fingers sliding to her hair. "Thank you."

"Oh!"

AT THE SURPRISED EXCLAMATION, Jess pulled back. Her stomach plummeted as she recognized the woman staring at them. "Oh."

"Dr. James? Giselle, remember?" The blonde placed a hand on her ample chest. "You came and helped my poor little Henrietta, remember?"

"Yes. Kind of hard to forget."

Tom snickered and Giselle's attention wandered to him. Then her eyes widened. "You! I know you, don't I?"

"Nope."

She squinted. "You play hockey, right? Oh my gosh. I knew Chad Pelley and Alex Kapaulenyuk. That was so sad when they left Calgary."

Mmm, from what she'd heard from Franklin it was more a case of good riddance to bad teammates.

"So, you two really are going out?"

Tom wrapped an arm around Jess's shoulders and kissed her cheek. "Yes."

"Aww! That's so sweet. Anyway, Dr. James—hold on. You're not related to Franklin James by any chance, are you?"

"He's my brother."

"Oh my gosh! That man is so hot! But I know he's married —"

"Yes, Hannah, his wife, is a good friend of mine."

"Ah. Well, okay."

"Have a good evening," Tom said.

"Oh, but before I go, Dr. James, is there any chance you can squeeze me in as one of your clients? I know you've got your own practice now, and little Henrietta really doesn't like her new vet. I'm afraid that maybe you were right, and her skin didn't like my hair dye, even though they promised it was all natural."

"You want me to do this after what you posted about me?"

"Look, I'm sorry. I mean, I really am. I was wrong, you were right. And look, I'm prepared to say that, and you know I have thousands of subscribers who would flock to see you if I posted how good you are."

"Thanks, but I have a very restricted clientele these days."

"*Very* exclusive," Tom added.

Jess bit back a smile. Exclusive because she was trying to have health boundaries and didn't want too many clients. She knew that comment would be like waving a red flag to this social climbing wannabe.

"Oh, but I *need* you. Please?"

Hmm. Giselle's eyes seemed genuine, but could she trust her?

Tom glanced at her, his expression saying she should be careful about letting this woman back into her world, and to be wise with her energy and hours. But the fact he said nothing said a lot. Like he trusted her to make the right call.

Her heart settled. "I can see about putting you on our waitlist, if space becomes available." That was the forgiving thing to do. Not promising was the wise thing to do.

"Oh, would you? I'd be *so* grateful."

"You should give her your card," Tom said to Giselle.

"My card? I don't have a card. Everyone always reaches out to me."

"That makes things tricky then. Oh well."

"No, wait. I'll write my details here." She scrabbled through her purse and found an old receipt. "Actually, I don't have a pen. Can I just send you my details via phone?"

"I prefer to not give out my number." Jess internally fist-pumped herself. Look at her, setting healthy boundaries.

"Then please put mine in yours. I *really* want to be on your wait list."

"It might take a while," Tom warned. "She's very popular."

"I know. I saw you two on the hockey dog run. Oh, is this your dog here?" She reached out a hand to Benji. "Hello, boy."

"Woof!"

"Oh!" Giselle scurried back. "He doesn't seem to like me."

Jess said nothing, but inwardly applauded her dog's discernment.

"Well, here is my number." Giselle's contact details were on a screen. "You can copy that in. I don't normally give my personal number out but seeing it's you."

"Take a photo, that'd be quicker," Tom suggested.

"Oh, thank you," Giselle gushed, as Jess did that. "I really hope to hear from you soon."

"Now, if you don't mind," Tom tugged Jess close again. "I really want to spend time with my girlfriend."

"Oh, okay, Sorry to bother you. Thanks again. Call me!"

Jess bit back a giggle as Giselle sashayed away, joining an older man.

"Will you call her?" Tom asked.

"Maybe. One day. If I'm desperate. I have forgiven her, just in case you're wondering. But I am trying to do better to keep the client list manageable."

"Yeah, she seems the kind of woman who doesn't like being managed."

"True. But still, it's my business to care about the animals, so I might find it in my heart to help poor little Henrietta."

"Do you only care about the animals? Or do you care about the owners too?" He nuzzled her neck.

She laughed and pushed him away. "Some of their owners."

"As long as it's this owner."

"Oh, it's always this owner." She traced his cheek, then leaned in for another kiss. Then another. Then—

"Ahem."

She startled, and retreated, and glanced up at their server. "Uh, hi."

"There seems to be a lot of that happening tonight." He handed them menus.

"That's weird," Tom murmured. "Imagine people kissing on Valentine's Day."

"I don't have to imagine it. I've seen plenty of it tonight." Their server's smile sagged as his eyes zeroed in on Tom. "Wait— you play for the Flames, right?"

She heard Tom's barely restrained sigh. "I do."

And sure enough, the man started singing the praises of the team, which didn't exactly contribute to romantic Valentine's Day vibes.

Fortunately, after taking their drinks orders, he soon left.

Tom turned to her. "I think that server needs to relax."

"He probably could do with one of your jokes."

Tom's head tilted. "Did you hear the one about the hockey player and the veterinarian?"

She smiled. "No."

"They met, became friends, had some challenges, got those sorted, then discovered how good it was to kiss each other."

"That doesn't sound like a joke. It sounds pretty serious to me."

"Oh, it is." He kissed her. "And this isn't a joke, either." He retrieved a little gift bag and slid it across the table.

Her heart skipped several beats. "You got me a present?" It

might be the most romantic day of the year, but she wasn't sure she was ready for what this jeweler's box-sized gift bag might contain. "I, uh, didn't get you anything."

"You organized dinner. Besides, your presence is gift enough for me."

A giggle escaped. "Oh my gosh. Cassie was right. You are beyond ready to be a dad with all these corny dad jokes."

"You let me know when you want that to happen, and I'll get two rings on your finger faster than you can say achoo."

SOMETIMES HIS MOUTH worked just a little quicker than his brain. "I meant—"

"It's okay. I know what you meant." Her smile held a promise that made his spirits soar. Then her face fell. "I hope Franklin can be a dad soon."

"They're doing okay."

Franklin had asked for prayer, and Tom had joined the others in the online Bible study group to pray for him. Hannah had taken some time off work, but was back now. Miscarriage was one of those things not talked about much, but it seemed like it shouldn't be considered shameful. But it was easy for him to say that, not having gone through the heartache of lost hopes and dreams. Even if he'd had a glimpse of what that might feel like this past year.

But those days were firmly behind them. "Go on, open it."

He watched as she lifted out a pink-wrapped box, ripped open the pink paper and finally slid open the velvet jewelry bag.

Her eyes, startled, turned to his. "Tom."

"Hey, it's not a ring. I don't want you getting disappointed."

Her cheeks pinked. "I wasn't—"

"One day though." He just figured this needed to come before that.

She tipped out a jewelry box and laughed. "This is like playing pass the present."

He watched as she opened the lid of the jewelry box. Her mouth opened, her eyes widened. "Oh, Tom."

When he'd asked Michelle and his mom what they recommended as a perfect Valentine's gift Michelle had suggested this. Well, not exactly this, but something along this line. Something elegant, for the woman who didn't often wear fancy clothes. Something expensive, that showed how much he valued her. And he'd figured this bit out himself: something that said how he truly felt about her.

She traced the silver heart pendant, with its movable diamond, the chain meaning she could wear it every day. His heart near hers.

"I could make some corny comment about how you have stolen my heart, or I've given you my heart, but I simply want to say..." He took a breath. "You're the best, most beautiful woman I know, and I love you, Dr. Jessica James."

"Oh, Tom." Her gaze lifted to his, her eyes rich and true. "I love you too."

His heart soared, and he leaned in to kiss her. Possessed her lips fully with his. She was beautiful and clever and everything he wanted. And he wanted her to know that one day—soon—he'd be happy to give her another diamond but this time on a—

"Ahem."

His eyes opened, and Jess pulled away, her shoulders slumping like she appreciated the interruption as little as he did.

"Have you had a chance to look at the menus?" their waiter asked.

"No. We need more time, thanks."

"Of course! Take as long as you need. But just not as long as Matthews' took to clear the goal in that last game. Can you believe he whiffed a shot and got scored on? Unbelievable."

No, what was unbelievable was this guy having no romance radar, on Valentine's Day, no less.

"Thanks." Jess's smile held an edge of exasperation. "We won't be too much longer."

"Oh, right. Of course. Let me know if I can help." He grinned and moved away, peeking back as if he couldn't quite believe Tom was sitting there.

Jess grimaced at Tom. "Sorry."

"What for? You're not responsible for a hockey-loving waiter."

Her nose wrinkled. "Is this what it'll always be like with you?"

He smiled, leaned closer. "I like the idea of 'always' with you."

Her eyes sparkled. "You really need to be careful with what you say. A girl could start getting ideas."

"What kind of ideas?" he murmured.

She didn't answer. Except that her smile that matched his, and the pink filling her cheeks, was a kind of answer. And he might be a little too faith-filled, but he'd like to think that those comments about forever were pretty positive signs that she'd be open to saying yes to a certain question he'd ask one day. Not today, but one day soon.

"Ahem."

Tom exhaled, and glanced up at their waiter. "Yes?"

"Decided yet?"

"No."

Maybe he bit that word a little sharply, for the waiter winced. "I'm really sorry for interrupting. But the kitchen is really busy, and I don't want my favorite hockey player to miss out."

Oh. His heart softened. He looked at the menu. Ordered the steak. Jess ordered the prosciutto-wrapped chicken.

"Excellent choices. And look, I'm sorry for butting in. I'd like to apologize by giving you desserts, on the house."

"You don't have to do that," Tom protested.

"Tom, if he's offering, you shouldn't say no." Jess's smile held a promise. "I'm quite fond of dessert, you know."

Tom snickered. He knew exactly what kind of sweet treat she was referring to.

"How about we see what dessert is on offer here?" Jess glanced at him.

The waiter blinked. "You want dessert before your mains?"

"Why not? Life is short. Eat dessert first."

"Very well. I'll talk to Chef."

She snuggled closer as their helpful waiter hurried to the kitchen. "You don't mind having dessert first, do you?"

"Depends on what kind of dessert we're talking about."

She laughed, and his heart filled with warmth. That sound was one of his favorites.

"It's free dessert, Tom. As long as chocolate is involved, it'll be okay. Besides, I'm prepared to overlook his interruptions as I know he's a fan of yours. Even though I'm a bigger one."

"Is that so?"

"Extremely so."

"You are most magnanimous."

"Want to see how magnanimous I can be?"

Oh, he liked this flirty side of hers. "Yes, I do."

"Okay." She shifted closer. Then caressed his cheek with her lips. "How's this?"

He closed his eyes. "That's more like it."

She moved to his mouth. "And this?"

"You kiss like a dream."

Benji gave a loud woof, which drew her laughter and his smile.

Their desserts soon arrived without any further Ahemming, and were deposited on the table with aplomb. And while Jess quickly spooned in some of the chocolate mousse, Tom barely cared about food, fixated as he was on his veterinarian with her smiles and soft laughter and the way her hand fitted in his.

"I meant it before," he said. "You are lovely to me."

"And you are sweeter than any dessert." She pressed her lips against his tenderly, her kiss tasting like chocolate and hope. "I'm so glad you didn't give up on me."

"I'm so glad you said yes."

"You said yes?" Their nosy waiter was back. "She said yes!"

"Oh my gosh." Jess blushed as the restaurant applauded, Giselle's eyes dinnerplate-sized as she lifted her phone as if taking a picture.

"Um, she said yes to going out with me," Tom tried to explain. "Not... what you mean."

"But if it makes you feel any better, I will say yes one day," Jess murmured.

"You will?" Tom asked quickly.

Her eyes shone. "I will."

And as her promise sank into his bones and he kissed her, his heart clenched anew at the fact this woman, his friend, had finally agreed to a future with him. Proof that she had always possessed a heart to help the needy, whether they be stray cats or dogs, or the man who had long known she was meant to be part of his life.

"Happy Valentine's Day."

"It's the happiest," she murmured. "You make me so happy."

He smiled, catching a sudden vision of a future blessed by God, blessed with love and life and laughter.

God was faithful, His plans were good. Tom kissed her knuckles. They would trust Him.

WANT to see who wins Poppy's heart? Find out in *A Second Chance for a Dancer*.

Thank you for reading *A Valentine for a Vet*, the second book in the Three Creek Ranch romance series, that follows *A Cameo for a Cowgirl*, and precedes *A Second Chance for a Dancer*. This is another of those 'accidental' series, where characters from *Fire and Ice* (Franklin and Hannah's story) took on a life off their own and demanded to have their stories told. So in this series we see Franklin's three sisters negotiate love and life and how that links to their family ranch.

Three Creek Ranch with its Western Town and Back Lot is actually based on a real ranch and movie set just outside Calgary, which has been the setting of all kinds of movies and TV shows, from *Lonesome Dove* to *Shanghai Noon* to *When Calls the Heart* and *Heartland*. I had *way* too much fun imagining what it must be like to manage a similar ranch and movie set, and have spent many an hour checking out the CL Western Town and Backlot site. It was super fun to first introduce the ranch in *Fire and Ice* and I can't wait to see this amazing place feature again in the last book in this series, *A Second Chance for a Dancer*, Poppy's story.

Readers who have been keeping up to date with my books may enjoy a few references to other characters, such as Lincoln Cash (who gets his own book in *Muskoka Spotlight,* which is part of the Muskoka Romance small town series), and Sylvie, who we got to know in *The Love Penalty*. And then there's Bree and Mike who we first met in *The Breakup Project* (which coincidentally, is where Franklin first gets his cameo too), the first book in the Original Six series. Oh, and to get some more Poppy fun, make sure you check out *Pointe, Shoots, and Scores.*

To find out more about these books and behind-the-scenes inspiration, and to sign up for my newsletter, please visit my website at www.carolynmillerauthor.com

Big thanks to May from Christian Shelves for her Canadian insights, and to Brittany, Shelene, Lisa, Judith, Evelyn and the other ladies in my ARC and review team.

Reviews help other readers find new-to-them authors, so if you can spare a moment to write a quick review at Amazon / Goodreads / your place of purchase, I'd be very grateful.

If you enjoy Christian contemporary romance you may want to check out the books in the Original Six hockey romance series, a sweet & swoony, slightly sporty Christian contemporary romance series.

The Breakup Project
Love on Ice
Checked Impressions
Hearts and Goals
Big Apple Atonement
Muskoka Blue

Romance fans who enjoy small town life may also enjoy reading the Muskoka Romance series, that starts with *Muskoka Shores.*

And if you need more small town stories, check out those in the Greener Gardens collections.

I'd love for you to check out my other books and to sign up for my newsletter at www.carolynmillerauthor.com where you can be the first to learn all my book and contest news, and discover more behind-the-book details and photos. Newsletter subscribers can also get an exclusive bonus book free, so grab your copy of *Originally Yours* here.

May God bless you - and happy reading!
Carolyn

About the Author

Carolyn Miller lives in the beautiful Southern Highlands of New South Wales, Australia, with her husband and four children. A longtime lover of romance, especially that of Jane Austen, Georgette Heyer and LM Montgomery, Carolyn loves to write contemporary and historical romance that draws readers into fictional worlds that show the truth of God's grace in our lives.

To find out more about Carolyn's books, and to subscribe to her newsletter, please visit www.carolynmillerauthor.com. By subscribing, you can also get a free novella, Originally Yours.

You can also connect with her at

ALSO BY CAROLYN MILLER

Contemporary:

The Original Six hockey series
The Breakup Project
Love on Ice
Checked Impressions
Hearts and Goals
Big Apple Atonement
Muskoka Blue

Northwest Ice hockey series
Fire and Ice
The Love Penalty
Pointe, Shoots, and Scores
Faking the Shot
Plays By the Book

Three Creeks Ranch Romance series
A Cameo for a Cowgirl
A Valentine for a Vet
A Second Chance for the Dancer

Muskoka Romance series
Muskoka Shores
Muskoka Christmas
Muskoka Hearts

Muskoka Spotlight

Muskoka Holiday Morsels

Muskoka Promise

Muskoka Miracle

<u>Trinity Lakes collection</u>

Love Somebody Like You

Tangled Up in Love

Only You Can Love Me

<u>Our House on Sycamore Street</u>

The Lost Daughter's Irishman

<u>The Fairall Romance Legacy</u>

An Irish Kiss

<u>The Greener Gardens Romance series</u>

Restoring Fairhaven

Regaining Mercy

Reclaiming Hope

Rebuilding Hearts

Refining Josie

<u>The Silver Teapot Series</u>

Not Exactly Mr Darcy

Not Precisely Mr Knightley

Historical:

<u>Regency Wallflowers</u>

Dusk's Darkest Shores

Midnight's Budding Morrow

Dawn's Untrodden Green

<u>Regency Brides: Legacy of Grace</u>

The Elusive Miss Ellison

The Captivating Lady Charlotte

The Dishonorable Miss DeLancey

<u>Regency Brides: Promise of Hope</u>

Winning Miss Winthrop

Miss Serena's Secret

The Making of Mrs Hale

<u>Regency Brides: Daughters of Aynsley</u>

A Hero for Miss Hatherleigh

Underestimating Miss Cecilia

Misleading Miss Verity

'Heaven and Nature Sing' from the Joy to the World Christmas
novella collection

'More than Gold' from

the Across the Shores novella collection

'Convincing the Circuit Preacher' from

The Courting the Country Preacher novella collection